Weavers Press San Francisco

The Great American Movie Script

Roshni Rustomji-Kerns

Weavers Press

San Francisco

https://weaverspress.wordpress.com/

Some of the narratives in THE GREAT AMERICAN MOVIE SCRIPT have been published earlier in different versions. "Rhodabeh" in Literary Review, Spring 1986, "Jerbanoo" in Toronto South Asia Review, 1986, "The Great American Movie Script" in CONTOURS OF THE HEART: SOUTH ASIANS MAP NORTH AMERICA eds. Rajini Srikanth and Sunaina Maira. Asian American Writers Workshop. Rutgers University Press. 1997, "How Roxanne Japanwallah Learned All About the Blues" in Toronto Journal of Writing Abroad, 2000, and "American Dhansak and the Holy Man of Oaxaca" in Massachusetts Review. 2004

This book would not have been possible without the help and support of patient readers and generous critics such as: Michael Carter, Charles Kerns, Flavia Krasilchik, Shabnam Nadiya, Shakira Rowyn, Moazzam Sheikh and, Karen Yamashita.

ISBN-13: 978-0984377626 (Weavers Press)
ISBN-10: 098437762X

Weavers Press is dedicated to publishing quality works of literature. Weavers Press prefers to publish works by and about South Asians but will consider other works as well if they tackle important issues or represent marginal voice.

For

*Charles Kerns, Elizabeth Parent, Victoria
Bomberry, and*

Glafira Salazar de Cruz

*with gratitude for their gift of the beloved tierra
and her stories*

Weavers Press San Francisco

Ancestors

Color Codified

"Sherman Alexie made me do it," she said.

It wasn't Sherman Alexie himself but a Thanksgiving Day radio interview with him she remembered having heard some years ago that made my friend Annie Foster demand that I tell her stories about my American ancestors. Especially stories about my ancestors that I was glad Sherman Alexie and Annie's ancestors hadn't killed off. "Even though your history in the Americas really doesn't go that far back," she conceded.

It was four months after Annie and I had returned from India when she began her "who are your American ancestors?" project.

She framed her question to me in the context of honoring my beloved dead. "In honor of our friend Homai Laura and your mother's friend, Ushabehen, and definitely in honor of your mother—all dead, of course. Tell me about your ancestors in America. If you don't know any stories about them, make up stories. It isn't all that difficult to do. Creating stories." She thought for about two and a half minutes, fished out the last bit of pistachio ice cream from the carton in her hand and said, "Sherman Alexie and your mother made me do it. They persuaded me to persuade you to talk about your American ancestors. Any of your ancestors from any part of the world who landed anywhere across America, this America—she be beautiful or not."

America beautiful or not. Ancestors in America.

My younger sister, Shireen, and I were in high school in Texas when she had tried to talk my mother into singing, "My Country 'Tis of Thee" and "America the Beautiful." My mother's response to Shireen's request was, "None of my fathers died in this country and America isn't the only beautiful land on earth." Shireen had insisted that there was no country as beautiful as America, "Beautiful in all ways," she had said.

I had told Annie about the mother-daughter patriotic songs' episode during one of our discussions, mutterings, conversations, questions, announcements that we indulged in constantly. Words, ideas, thoughts that meandered through

Indians from Americas such as Annie, Indians from India such as I

supposed brown/supposed red

what does it mean for immigrants from Asia to aid and abet European settlers and

colonizers of the Americas

white on brown, brown on black, shades of brown on imagined red and

"let me count the ways" that of course was Annie, "to throttle people when they ask, 'Are you a sheet-wearing or blanket-wearing Indian?'"

And now many years later, Annie was connecting Shireen's request for the two songs and my mother's response to a Sherman Alexie NPR interview.

Ancestors. America, beautiful or not.

As far as Annie was concerned, I, Rhoda Sohrabji, was to stop "meddling with numbers and start learning how to put words together. Stop counting. Start telling. Sing me America. Sing me your ancestors." At my horrified look, Annie said, "OK, no singing. Tell me. Write me the stories. Words not numbers. THAT will help you accept who you are." I told her that she sounded like a self-help guru.

Annie changed her argument. She claimed that stories about American ancestors were absolutely necessary for her to begin working on her long procrastinated dream, The Great American Movie Script project.

Instead of a whale—white or otherwise—riding the seas, my literature-saturated friend Annie planned to have an enormous flag—stars and stripes—floating across the oceans of the world while her ancestors waved farewell to it from their homes in Alaska. The flag would sing about halls of Montezuma, shores of Tripoli and places where buffaloes no longer roam. Please do not ask me how Annie was going to accomplish all of this in her Great American Movie Script. I asked her but she just said, "Wait and see." When I asked her if the "Great" described America or her Script, she merely glared at me and muttered something about clueless mathematicians.

At the time of the Sherman Alexie interview, which I didn't hear, I was retired from Sierra College in Northern California. The Vietnam War vets to whom I had taught calculus were now trying to teach a younger generation of students to stay out of the latest United Statesian Wars of Salvation.

According to Annie, the NPR interviewer had asked Sherman Alexie if he was thankful for anything on Thanksgiving Day. Sherman Alexie had answered that he was thankful his ancestors hadn't slaughtered Bruce Springsteen's ancestors.

Annie compiled a list of all the Americans from what she calls "Ye Olde Already Discovered Worlde" whose ancestors she was grateful her ancestors hadn't killed off. It wasn't a long list. It included

> ancestors of Eleanor Roosevelt
> ancestors of Ava Gardner
> ancestors of Marlon Brando
> ancestors of Anne Richards
> ancestors of Joan Baez

ancestors of Herman Melville
ancestors of Willie Nelson and
ancestors of Ben and Jerry.

Annie has been known to say that the only good thing the Europeans brought to the Americas was ice cream. Ice cream according to Annie is "the epitome of the culture of Ye Olde Already Discovered Worlde." She changed her mind when many years later she tasted pistachio kulfi from the Parsi Dairy Farm vendor in a train going from Mumbai to Pune. But since kulfi hasn't been easily available in the Americas until quite recently, she felt that it wouldn't be honest to include ancestors of American kulfiwalas in her list. Maybe it could be considered after at least one and a half generations of South Asian American kulficrafters.

After trying to enlist me, Annie sent her list of "I am glad my ancestors didn't kill these people's ancestors" to an assorted group of her friends and relatives in various parts of the world and asked them if in order to be a true American ancestor, a person had to be born AND to die, to be buried or scattered in any part of the earth or waters of the Americas. Or, she asked, could someone qualify as an American ancestor if someone not born in the Americas merely died and was buried or scattered somewhere in the Americas.

Annie might have been thinking once again of my mother when she wondered about birth, death and burial. My mother, Nergiz Japanwallah, was born in Mumbai in 1915. She married my father, Rustom Sohrabji in 1936. My mother died in 1987. Before the Sherman Alexie interview and Annie's obsession with ancestors.

My father was born in Pune in 1914. He died in 2007 a few years after Annie's project was launched. He was intrigued by Annie's questions and wondered if Annie would be willing to drop the idea of the flag and keep the white whale intact. He requested that regardless of a monocolored whale or a multicolored flag, could Annie please redeem the Parsi from Melville's delusions regarding people of ancient, "exotic, evil" religions? He also wondered if Annie could somehow correct Melville's Islam/Zoroastrian confusion. Fedallah. "A Parsi character whose name has no Hormuzd in it but includes Allah? A name is a name is a name regardless of how someone smells." My father was also a literature-leaning person. Annie had to explain the last part of my father's request to me.

Annie's brother Max sent an email from somewhere in West Asia explaining that anyone who wanted to claim American ancestorhood should be granted that title. "American," he said. "Not United Statesian or Mexican or Brazilian or Paraguayan or a specific nation space. Just American." Max remains a dreamer. He dreams of world peace. That is what he talks about all the time because he says that he still dreams of the people of Vietnam he killed during the war. He doesn't know if the people he killed were from the North or the South or even if they were soldiers. "Vietnamese people" he says, "I killed people. From the North, from the South, it doesn't matter from what part of the land."

When Annie asked for their stories, her father, William Foster, and his friend, my father, Rustom Sohrabji, began by indulging in convoluted conversations between the two of them over the phone and through the US Postal Service. California to Alaska. Alaska to California. They talked about ancestors and first human beings in general not only in the Americas but on earth. Metamorphosing fish and toads and dinosaurs and spiritual entities entered their discussions.

My cousin a few times removed, Roxanne Japanwallah, who happens to be a good friend of Annie's, sent her response from India through email. "Anyone who can sing all the verses of that 'bombs bursting in air' song without breaking on the high notes should be able to claim United Statesian ancestors."

My friend Erach Wadia phoned from Oaxaca. He, of

course, wanted to know what Annie meant by American and could he, born in India, claim Benito Juarez as an ancestor? His request to claim Benito Juarez as an ancestor was based rather dubiously on a supposed similarity between one of his great-aunts and Benito Juarez. His great-aunt, a Satyagrahi, had followed Gandhiji on the Salt March and was said to have always covered her "wheat brown" face and arms with a generous amount of white face powder whenever she had to be at a public function where there were British and later, United Statesian sahibs and memsahibs. Benito Juarez was rumored to do the same when he made public appearances.

Annie didn't have an opportunity to ask my mother's friend, Ushabehen, of Texas about American ancestors. Because as I mentioned, Ushabehen was already dead. Annie's friend, Homai Laura Sethna of California was also dead. If they could have responded to Annie, Ushabehen would have sung about Mumbai, meri jaan and her adopted grandchild from Cambodia. Homai would have started a socio-historical discussion of "that green patina on white whatever-covered" Statue of Liberty asking for the poor and the hungry of the world.

When Annie asked me for "ancestors in the Americas stories", I said I didn't think I could help her because questions of ancestors, nationalities and who belonged where have never interested me. I did not to tell her that questions such as these frighten me.

Annie was insistent. She talked about if not now and what about then and the present, past and future. "We mustn't forget our stories. If we do, we will be destroyed." She somehow brought in Euripides and his belief that those of us whom the Gods wish to destroy, they first try to drive mad. It was the same quote Annie had recited to me when she described to me what one of her supposedly "well-meaning" professors at the four year college she had attended—pre-UC Berkeley—had said to her in order to thwart her "ambition to get a graduate degree from a BIG, important university such as UC Berkeley." The professor had thought to dissuade Annie from the pitfalls of ambition with the warning—delivered, according to Annie "with an amazing depth of thoughtlessness which passes as kindness" —that Annie should reassess her UC Berkeley dream. "Because" the professor had said, "you will find a university such as UC Berkeley extremely difficult. They will demand very hard work from you." Annie was trying not to shout as she asked me, "Hard work? Hard work! She speaks of hard work to me? Me, am I their proverbial lazy Indian? They first try to drive us mad—yes, I am mad as in anger—not as in insanity—sorry Mr. Myth-changing Euripides—and then they try to destroy us. All in the name of helping us. "

Annie continued to explain her insistence on my delving into the "ancestor-project" because she said that the time had arrived to work seriously on her Great American Movie Script." It will be a collaboration" she said. "Stories from my friends, relatives, strangers. Stories of ancestors dead and/or alive. And you, Rhoda will start me off."

I reminded her once again that I am a mathematician. A retired teacher of numbers. Words were my mother's weapon and she was dead.

And like a demented, determined, wingless angel holding the ice-cream spoon as if it were some kind of a virtual flaming pen, an Indian-calendar Ganesha with his tusk dipped in celestial ink, Annie waved her arm wildly, threatening to dislodge the photo of my sister, Shireen, placed carefully on the green, upright piano in my kitchen in Pescadero and demanded, "Write!"

Political Demonstrations and Personal Letters
Red and Brown and In Between

Although Annie Foster and I met in the late sixties during an anti-war march in Berkeley, we didn't become good friends until we exchanged our stories about green Jello. Specifically, green Jello with fruit cocktail. By "good friends," I mean friends who become the kind of "by blood" family unit that usually exists only in sentimental novels, TV shows or in the wishful imagination of an alarming number of human beings. The type of friends who reach a level of comfort that allows for the intensity of disagreements or of love only very few family members can afford to live within.

Before the green Jello-definitely-with-fruit incident, Annie Foster and I used our separate birth places, hers being her Aunt Mabel's home in Bethel, Alaska, USA, and mine being the Parsi Lying-In Hospital in Mumbai, India; our mother-languages, hers being Yupik Eskimo, mine being Gujarati; and our supposedly insurmountable cultural differences to keep us from forming a not-bonded-by-blood family unit. Although she and I were both born on October 31, she in 1935 and I in 1937, although both of us considered Northern California our home and although quite soon after we met, she and I did become related by one of the more traditional methods, the marriage of our siblings, we didn't really feel at home with one another until at least seven months after we met.

When Annie and I found ourselves walking next to one another during that anti-war march, we looked at the placard that each of us was carrying as we marched along Telegraph Avenue. Right there in front of God and everybody including Berkeley police officers and FBI agents. Both placards said, "An Indian

Woman against America's War against Vietnam."

"You," said Annie, "are from India. I am Annie Foster from Alaska. A Yupik. When I left home and came to California, I decided that I too was an Indian. A Native American. An indigenous woman. My brother insists that he is Yupik and not Indian. But then he never did get involved with the AIM. Instead he went to Vietnam. I try not to be overly anxious about the identity police permeating this land."

"I," said I, "was born in India but have lived in America since I was five years old. My name is Rhoda, short for Rhodabeh, Sohrabji, and I am against this war. My sister is not against the war at all. To prove her point, she is in Vietnam as an army nurse. She would have preferred to go there as a combatant. She is quite ferocious, this sister of mine. A healer who would rather be a warrior."

Annie smiled and her eyes turned from black to amber and back again to black—or maybe it was amber. I found out later that her eyes change black-amber-black whenever she finds the world amusing or terrifying. She denies that her eyes change colors.

Annie announced that she was against any and all wars. "I don't know if my brother is against or for the war. But he is there. The draft did it. At one time, he announced that he would be a priest. But now he is a warrior and I have been reduced to praying for his safety."

I didn't tell Annie that from the day my sister had left for Vietnam, my mother had called me every morning from our home outside of Dallas. To tell me that she had just awakened from a dream that assured her that Shireen was alive and well. Annie didn't mention to me until later that she too kept an eye on her brother's welfare in Vietnam through her dreams. One doesn't talk with any sense of ease about such things in America. When I refuse to tell my mother about my dreams, she shakes her head sadly and says, "Rhodabeh, if we were still at home, in India, you would tell me your dreams. No one there thinks that such discussions are private or silly or crazy." I was not sure if that was still true of India. Neither my mother nor my father nor Shireen nor I had been in India, since 1944. We had made that 1944 visit for the Navjote ceremony in Bombay in which my younger sister and I were officially initiated into our Zoroastrian faith. I don't have many memories from that visit. Except that it was in Bombay—my mother always called it Mumbai—where I, brought up in Dallas, Texas, fell in love with the ocean.

When Annie and I left the Berkeley demonstration, we exchanged addresses and phone numbers and made vague noises about keeping in touch.

Three weeks after we met, Annie sent me a cartoon she had cut out of a newspaper. About seven people, women and men, in various versions of Hollywood style "Indian costumes" were welcoming Christopher Columbus to their island. The leader of the welcoming party was holding up a placard that read, "We thank the Great Spirit for sending you to us. Ever since the Great Spirit created our land and our people, we have been lost because we have not known what to call ourselves. Now we know! We are Indians." Annie had written, on top of the cartoon, "Hallelujah! Hallelujah! And Adam named the animals etc. This would make a great beginning for my movie script!"

I phoned Annie to ask about her movie script statement and that was when I learned that her ambition since she was eight years old has been to write the Great American Movie Script.

After she sent me the cartoon, we met for coffee every few weeks to exchange news about our lives as graduate students at UC Berkeley. We discussed the war in Southeast Asia in general terms, but we never spoke about the presence of our siblings in that area of the world until the day, about seven months later, when she called me and said, "We need to meet as soon as possible. Can you please meet me in front of Dwinelle Hall tomorrow morning? Early?" I had already left a message for her which she hadn't received, "Annie, we must meet as soon as possible. Tomorrow at 9 a.m. in front of Dwinelle?"

We met at 8.30 the next morning at Sather Gate. Both of us with two letters in our hands. She said, "What is your sister's name?" "Shireen," I said. She gave me one of her letters. I had already started with, "What is your brother's..." when I remembered her mentioning her brother "Max." I handed her one of my letters. And of course, my sister and her brother had met and married in Vietnam. As my cousin, the-famous-detective-lawyer of Devinagar, India, Roxanne Japanwallah, would say, "Things like that happen to happen. Especially if you are a Sohrabji or a Japanwallah. Coincidences keep the world spinning at the correct angle on its axis."

Annie and I were informed, she by her brother, I, by my sister that they had met two months ago, somewhere in Vietnam. We were further informed that at that first meeting, Shireen had yelled at Max that neither he nor she were Indians, they were Americans. He had smiled and quoted from the *Bhagvadgita*. Shireen, who seldom read, was persuaded by Max to read the *Gita* and was immediately impressed by its code of duty. Max had tried to explain the complications that could arise from such a code. Shireen had disagreed with him and in the process fallen in love with him. And he with her. The two of them, of course, had no idea that Annie and I had met during our efforts to end the war and bring them home to the States as soon as possible.

Many years later, a few days before she died, my mother remembered how Shireen and Max had met. She shook her head and said, "Those poor children. They didn't realize how beautifully dangerous the *Gita* is!"

When Annie and I read those first letters announcing the Shireen-Max marriage, we grinned at one another. Annie's eyes turned from black to amber to black. I said, "We are sisters-in-law, or some such thing. We should celebrate."

But then we both stopped grinning. She and I exchanged the second letters we had received.

Hers was from her father. It said: "Dear Annie—By now Max must have written to you to tell you that he has married an Indian woman. From India. In Vietnam. Why couldn't he, my only son, have married a real American woman? There are American women even in Vietnam.

"I have nothing against Indians from India but what will happen to my grandchildren? Max's children? What will Max's wife know anything about us? About our ways? What will happen if her family looks down upon us and thinks that we exist only in history books or movies?

"You know that our Max will have exceptionally wonderful children. Beautiful, healthy, smart. And I am afraid that his wife's family will not let us keep our grandchildren. And even if I will be allowed to teach them our ways, they will insist on making them as Asian as possible. The Asians don't like to lose their children to other cultures. And I don't blame them. And in that other war, when I went to Japan, did I marry an Asian woman? No. I came back and married a woman of my own people! We can't afford to lose any more of our children. You of all people know that better than most others. Why couldn't your brother have just married an American? If not from our own people, at least a born-in-America American. Some of those younger people are learning to respect our culture and our ways.

"Your Aunt Mabel is driving me crazy. More than usual crazy. She is very happy about the marriage. She keeps on talking about how she has dreamed that Max will be very happy in this marriage. I would be happier if he married an American woman. And if I were assured that my grandchildren will be counted among us. Alaska Natives. Yupik. But it has happened differently and that's how it is. Love, Dad"

I turned to Annie and said, "But Shireen is an American. She came here when she was four. She is more American than most of my born-in-the United States of America friends! At one time, when she was about seven years old, she was so insistent about proving herself and us, her family, as "real" Americans that she forced us to recite the Pledge of Allegiance every Friday evening before dinner. We pledged allegiance for about three weeks before we rebelled. To compensate for our rebellion and to assure her that we were Americans, my parents bought an American flag and stuck a flag pole in the middle of our front lawn. And they hoisted that flag not only on all the patriotic holidays but also on Shireen's birthday. They still fly that flag on special occasions."

Annie shook her head. "I hear they do such things in Texas. That is a movie script I didn't write! But I don't know about my father, Rhoda. Our siblings are barely married and my father is already talking about grandchildren. Oh well! It will be my job to begin educating him about Indians, from India, in America. Somehow I will persuade him that Shireen is an American. I am not sure if the Pledge of Allegiance and the flag will quite work out. Even though he was in the army and all that, he has mixed feelings about the American government and their insistence on presenting us with the American flag to celebrate any and all events.

"Frances Scott Key composed 'The Star Spangled Banner' on the *Minden*. . ." I began to say. Annie cut me off.

"I know that."

"But you didn't know that the ship was built in Bombay for the British by the Wadias. Parsi master shipbuilders."

Annie looked mildly interested. "I don't know if that will help either. But I know that your sister being a warrior—a healer and a warrior—will work well. But what about your father, Rhoda? Red Indians?? Some educating of your father is needed!"

She had just read the letter my father had sent me.

My father had written that he was extremely upset about Shireen's marriage to Max. He said that he was proud and happy to be in America. The best place on earth. But what was the use of being in America, in the New World, with two healthy children when one, namely I, was turning out to be a nimak-haram, a betrayer of the salt given to us by the country which had taken us in and given us so much? That, of course, was in reference to my anti-war stand. My father had portraits of every single President of the United States, from George Washington onwards, on the walls of the waiting room of his dental office.

After expressing his disappointment in how I had "turned out", my father went on to write about Shireen's marriage. He was extremely proud of her for having volunteered to take care of "our boys in Vietnam" who were protecting democracy and America in that far way Asian land. But now she had gone ahead and gotten married without telling her parents about her plans. That didn't upset him as much as the fact that she had married not a Parsi, as was expected of her, but an outsider. Were there Parsis in the American forces in Vietnam? Most probably. But she had not found a Parsi to marry there in Vietnam nor had she waited to come back home, to America, to find a Parsi husband.

"I would have taken her to Bombay, Karachi, Puna or even Devinagar," wrote my father, "to find a good Parsi boy for her, if she so desired. It is an offer I have made so often to you. An offer you won't even consider. But Rhodabeh, if Shireen chose to marry outside our faith, outside our community, why didn't she marry a real, regular American? I don't think your mother and I have ever even met a Red Indian. Shireen says he is a Yupik Eskimo. A Native American. Why is this man in Vietnam? I thought they all live on reservations. I do honor him for fighting for his country and I am sure he is a very nice man. He wrote a very respectful letter to us about how much he loved Shireen and how he will take care of her.

"But I ask you, Rhodabeh, who will perform the Navjote ceremonies for Shireen's children? You know that it is hard to find a mobed who will perform the Navjote for a child of a Zoroastrian Parsi woman married to a non-Zoroastrian. Your mother and I think that is not at all correct. Some of our Parsis are getting so conservative about our girls marrying outside the community and the Navjotes for their children and all that. And if there are no Navjotes for the children born to our Shireen, will her children, my grandchildren, be counted as Parsis, Jarthoshtis? Even if you, Rhodabeh, don't care about our dwindling numbers—less than 10,000 of us and getting fewer!. . .I care very much. I am very disturbed by all this, I tell you. Will we be able to find a mobed willing to perform our ancient Jarthoshti sudreh-kusti ceremony for my grandchildren when he finds out that the father is a Red Indian? We don't know what religion he follows. Will Shireen's husband and his family allow the children to become Zoroastrians?

"I tell you Rhodabeh," my father never calls me Rhoda when he is upset, "I try to be tolerant and open-minded. After all, we are all children of God but we can't afford to lose our ancient faith and our children.

"Your mother, as usual, is not worried. She says she is happy for Shireen and that Max Foster sounds like a very nice man. She wants to meet his family as soon as possible. I don't want to go to Alaska. So please persuade your mother not to go overboard about this marriage. I will try to make the best of this situation. We will just tell people that Shireen has married a soldier in the American army in Vietnam. When we see what he looks like and find out what he believes in, we will decide if we need to tell people that he is not quite a real, regular American. Love, Daddy"

Annie's Aunt Mabel and my mother persuaded the two

fathers to calm down. And anyway, the two fathers need not have concerned themselves about grandchildren. The US army informed us that Shireen was missing. They were sure my sister Shireen had died in Vietnam seventeen months after she and Max got married. Shireen's body was not sent to us because the army couldn't find her body.

My mother and Aunt Mabel continued to report dreams in which Shireen was still alive. Somewhere in Asia. Trying to remember who she was so she could return home. I told my mother that dreams are messy, inelegant and undependable. My mother shook her head and laughed. And as always when she laughed, she covered her mouth with her left hand. The brown hand with the puckered up skin and the pink verging on yellow scars she always said would fade as she got older. It was the hand her British teacher in Mumbai had slammed into a desk drawer when my mother had announced that Shakespeare was not the most important writer in the world. Shakespeare, according to my eleven year old mother, may have been ONE of the important writers of the world. Together with Kalidasa and Tagore and Valmiki and, yes, Homer. My mother's family had educated her well. My mother's British teacher didn't approve of that kind of an education. My mother wore the scars of her British teacher's attempt at educating her till the day she died.

Shireen's death brought Max's father to Texas to be with my father. And although the two men remained close friends for the rest of their lives, my father never visited Alaska. At first, they wrote long letters to one another about the importance of keeping up traditions and the old ways. Max who continued to keep in touch with my mother through letters and long phone calls said that the two fathers should go down in history. His father-in-law as the only Parsi who knew as much as a non-Alaska Native could know about Yupik Eskimos and his father as the first Yupik Eskimo scholar of Zoroastrianism.

After Annie and I graduated, Annie became a freelance journalist and writer of mystery novels. She bought a condo in San Francisco. I was hired as an Assistant Professor in the mathematics department at Sierra College in San Mateo and lived in Pescadero. The Pacific Ocean was only a fifteen minute walk from my home.

Green Jello with Fruit
The Persistence of Color

After we graduated from Berkeley, Annie and I tried to meet every Friday evening at Duarte's Restaurant in Pescadero. I wasn't overly worried when Annie didn't show up one Friday evening in August. Her work, both as a journalist and a writer of mysteries, often forced her to take off to strange places at a moment's notice.

Annie called me the next day at 11 a.m. She had just been discharged from the hospital where she had spent the night after an accident on her way to Duarte's. She had been too drugged and too much in pain to call me earlier. I told her not to move from her bed until I arrived at her door and asked if she needed anything.

"Yes," she said, "Can you please bring me something to eat? I am very hungry and there is nothing of great interest in my refrigerator. And I am not bedridden just a bit shaken up."

"What would you like to eat?" I asked her.

"If it isn't too much trouble, that spicy chicken you make. Or any other type of chicken. Except the Colonel's. Any spicy food. And Green Jello with fruit cocktail. Actually what I want the most right now is that Green Jello with fruit in it. With maybe ice cream on the side. Vanilla or pistachio."

I didn't say anything.

When my silence continued, Annie sounded irritated. "What's the matter? Do you have something against Jello with fruit cocktail?

"No. It's just that I have never made it. I don't like it."

"Rhoda! Jello is the easiest thing in the world to make. You can also buy it in that deli near your house. You don't have to eat it. Bring yourself some cookies or something. Right now, your company and Green Jello with fruit cocktail will go a long way to make me feel better. My special comfort food and another Indian is what I need now. That stupid car just plowed right into my car. Forget about the ice cream. I think I already have some in my freezer."

I took the chicken dhansak I had frozen for emergencies. Emergencies such as when Annie would show up at my house and request, "good, hot and spicy Parsi food. Shrimp stew or chicken dhansak." She had learned the names of the few Parsi dishes I cooked when I missed my mother. I had warned her that I didn't do "authentic" only nostalgic. She didn't seem worried about that.

The green Jello with fruit cocktail that I bought at the deli was quite festive. Christmassy green and perfectly molded with precisely placed curves. Yellow, green and red fruit appeared at careful intervals inside the gelatin and four bright red maraschino cherries were perched outside on the crown. A container of whipped cream accompanied the whole production.

After we ate, I insisted on Annie coming with me to my house and staying with me for a few days. She brought the left-over portion of the green Jello to my house together with her typewriter. She spent the weekend with me and one afternoon, taught me how to make Jello with fruit cocktail. I requested that it be red, not green, Jello. Her eyes had done their color-turning trick about three times during the Jello cooking lesson.

The day after that cooking lesson, Annie woke up looking quite upset and retreated into my office. I heard her typing for at least two hours. I wondered if the accident had inspired her at last to begin her Great American Movie Script.

Later that evening she showed me what she had written.

Annie had written an article about her accident in which she credited her quick recovery to me, her sister-in-law-of-sorts, Rhodabeh—Rhoda for short—Sohrabji and green Jello with fruit cocktail. And then she discussed, not quite briefly, how she, who prided herself on always being alert to cultural differences, had "blown it" with me. She, Annie, had demanded her own culturally defined comfort food, green Jello with fruit cocktail, from me who didn't have the same comfort foods. I, who obviously didn't even like that dessert, had to first buy the Jello from a deli and then be persuaded to buy a packet of red Jello and learn to make it in my own kitchen. Annie wrote that she had forgotten that Jello, a food that is basic, easy to prepare and pretty good to eat as far as many Americans are concerned, may not be basic, easy or tasty for many other Americans such as her "transposed from India" friend and relative, Rhoda Sohrabji.

"I couldn't, of course, include the dream I had the night before the accident. One doesn't do such things in newspaper articles." Annie said to me. "I saw Shireen sitting with us at Duarte's Tavern. Shireen turned to me and said, 'Annie, don't worry too much about me. Very soon you will be on your way to Asia.' What do you think about that, Rhoda? As you know, I really don't like to travel much. I leave that to Max."

After being discharged—honorably—Max had become what he termed "a peace and justice union organizer" and traveled not only all across the United States but also to other countries to work with anti-war, anti-colonial organizations. Annie kept on saying that he would end up being a "crazy Buddhist-Sufi-Unitarian-liberation priest."

When Annie asked me what I thought about her dream, I wanted to talk about more tangible matters. Such as the two blue herons I had seen in the Pescadero marsh the week before. Such as my looking forward to the annual visit of the red-tailed hawk that swoops down—once, twice, three times—in my backyard at the beginning of fall. Such as the astonishing green-gray color of the ocean the day before as it retreated from Pescadero Beach at low tide. As I began to talk about these matters of the earth and the ocean, I decided it was time to tell Annie the story about

Shireen, myself and green Jello with fruit cocktail.

"Do you want to know why I don't like green Jello, with or without fruit?" I asked Annie.

"Not your ethnic, cultural comfort food. And you didn't grow up on US Government Issue food the way I did."

"None of the above." I said. I had never told anyone else, not even my mother about the green Jello. I wondered if Shireen had told Max about our Sunday with Judy Taylor during which green Jello played a crucial role.

When I was eight years old and Shireen was about six, my best friend of that year, Judy Taylor, invited us to spend a Sunday with her and her family.

Shireen and I didn't know that we were expected to attend church with the Taylors or that Mr. Taylor was a Minister. My sister and I, of course, knew something about the Christian story. And we were vaguely aware that in Christian churches the Minister preached and prayed and everybody in the church prayed and sang. But neither of us had ever attended a church before. Our first experience was in a church where we were the only two non-white, non-Christian people in the congregation. The church was presided over by Mr. Taylor. A friendly, funny, gentle man whenever we had met him at our school events, he became a born-again, fire-and-brimstone preacher in that church. And he pitched his sermon at us. "Two little heathen girls," he said—and he said it very loudly. "He couldn't believe it! Heathens in America! In American schools! His heart wept for us. He knew that his little daughter, Judy, had befriended us because God had sent a message to her to befriend us and to bring us to her father's church." Judy whispered to me that she had befriended me because I could help her with math. Judy detested anything that involved numbers. She preferred words and pictures. Mr. Taylor, of course, didn't hear her. He went on to state that his mission in life was to save people such as the two little visitors in his church. He wanted to save two such sweet, well-behaved little girls from the terrors of hell.

Mr. Taylor spoke. The congregation prayed with him and then all of them stood up and sang hymns. Shireen and I also stood up but of course neither of us knew the songs. I tried to hum along because I really liked the sound of some of the songs. I had stopped listening to Mr. Taylor after about the first five minutes. He was so loud that he hurt my ears and I was fascinated by the hat the lady in front of me was wearing. It had birds and flowers and a huge yellow bow. I wondered what my mother, who always wore saris, would look like in such a fantastic hat. Judy whispered to me that the hat was ugly and old-fashioned and the lady who was wearing it was a witch. A real witch. She baked cakes that put children to sleep and sent them to hell for ten years—at least. I didn't believe her but I saw Shireen shudder.

Shireen had been paying attention to every single word of that sermon and was terrified. Since I hadn't really heard much more after Mr. Taylor's statement about saving us from the terrors of hell, and since I rather liked Mr. Taylor and wasn't particularly terrified by hell, I didn't know what to say or do to make Shireen lose that look of a hunted rabbit as we came out of the church.

Mr. Taylor's sermon continued during lunch at Judy's house. But now, Mr. Taylor was back to his gentle, sweet self. He spoke softly. He patted our heads and hands while he spoke. And Shireen became more and more agitated. She pushed her mashed potatoes all around her plate. She barely ate the fried chicken as she listened to Mr. Taylor. She stopped eating completely when he pulled out a dollar bill and said, "America is God's country. A Christian country. See? Young lady, read out aloud what it says here!" He held the dollar under Shireen's nose and pointed a bit above the picture of George Washington. Shireen who always spoke loudly and clearly, stuttered as she read, "In God We Trust."

"Yes," said Mr. Taylor. "One God. The God. The God of our fathers. Jesus Christ the Son of God who died so we, all of us, can be saved. And this is a good Christian country. And the two of you are very good little girls. But how can you be true Americans if you are not Christians?" And he put another piece of chicken and another dollop of mashed potatoes on Shireen's plate. He didn't seem to notice that she had tears running down her face as he asked his wife for a cup of coffee.

Mrs. Taylor went off to the kitchen to get the coffee and I tried to distract Shireen by pointing at the dessert in the middle of the round table covered with a pale blue, very delicate lace table cloth. Shireen loved desserts and the color blue. The dessert in the middle of the table was green Jello with pieces of bright colored fruit stuck inside it.

Judy and I watched with awe, as Judy's baby sister who was sitting on a high chair, began to take advantage of her mother's absence. She reached over and started to pull off globs of that green Jello. Some of it did find its way into the little girl's mouth but most of it was smeared, with immense concentration and satisfaction, all over her face and into her hair. Mr. Taylor didn't seem to notice anything his little daughter was doing.

Mrs. Taylor returned to the dining table and looked at her baby daughter and my sister with dismay. She picked up a napkin and began wiping the Jello from the little girl's face who set up quite a lamentation. Then Mrs. Taylor tried to dry my sister's tears with the same napkin. My sister continued to cry silently. While she was wiping off the Jello and the tears, Mrs. Taylor spoke to her daughter and Shireen. "There, there, Shireen. You naughty little girl. . .not you Shireen. . .but Shireen there is nothing to cry about honey! Don't be afraid. Mr. Taylor is trying to help you and Rhoda. He is trying to give you a wonderful gift. Just listen to him, honey. There is nothing to fear about Christianity. No, you may not have any more Jello." The last, of course, to her little daughter.

Mrs. Taylor didn't realize that it wasn't Christianity that was terrifying Shireen into tears. It was the whole question of being an American, a good American, a real American that was scaring my sister.

Shireen was obsessed by the idea of being an American. The Monday before that Sunday lunch, she had come home covered with mud, her clothes torn, a bruise on her right cheek and dried blood around her nose. One of her classmates, Gloria Allen, had told Shireen that she wasn't a real American because Shireen was dark and wasn't a Christian. Gloria had suggested that if Shireen drank lots and lots of milk and took at least three showers a day, her complexion might improve. She also suggested that Shireen tell our parents to look for a Christian church where we could worship. Her church didn't like to have "colored people," or foreigners attending services. Shireen didn't mind the milk part but she hated water in the form of showers, baths, swimming pools. She didn't know what to make about the church part.

My sister didn't begin the fight until Gloria told her that we, all of us, were uncivilized. We didn't always speak English in our home and my mother wore strange clothes. Apparently Shireen hit out when Gloria told her that her uncle said that all of us foreigners should be deported.

Shireen started crying as soon as she came home. "Mummy," she sobbed, "where will we go when they deeeport us? I don't want to go anywhere else. I like Dallas. I like Texas. I like America. We will be without a home!" And then she hid her face in our mother's lap and said, "Please, please Mummy, please don't wear saris anymore. Not outside the house. I love you very much but please don't wear saris! And I promise I will take two showers a day. Every day."

I don't know who had won the Shireen vs. Gloria fight but I do know that it took my mother at least two hours to clean and calm my sister. Trying to calm Shireen's fear, she said, "If they deport us, we could go to Mexico. My friend Señora Rachel and her family in Oaxaca will help us." My mother had met Señora

Rachel at the local Post Office. Their friendship was based on their shared mistrust of government agencies and their shared belief that no human being was a stranger to either of them.

My mother's suggestion about Mexico was dismissed by my sister Shireen. I was intrigued by the idea of a world beyond Texas. I wanted to go to Mexico. I also wanted to go to Vienna because I had read that they had the world's best pastries. My father said, "Shireen, stop your melodrama. Making a tamasha of everything that happens. No one is going to deport us."

Shireen remained unconvinced.

To return to that Sunday lunch at Judy's house, Shireen's terror about being "deeeported" was being intensified by Mr. Taylor's efforts to help us with his official and unofficial sermon about Christianity and being a true American.

Mr. Taylor looked at his wife with the napkin in her hand and noticed Shireen's tears. "Little girl," he said, "Don't cry. Don't you like chicken and potatoes? Don't worry. You don't have to eat them. Here take some Jello. It's really good."

Mrs. Taylor carefully carved us Jello servings from the side that had not been demolished by her daughter. Judy said that the gouged-out mound of Jello reminded her of Mount Rushmore. Shireen stopped crying and ate the dessert. It may have been the last time that she and I ate green Jello with fruit cocktail.

Annie laughed at my story. "What a script! I don't blame you. Definitely not in the comfort food category for you and Shireen."

There was more to the story.

A few days later, while Shireen was still trying to get over her fear of hell and "deeeportation," the Allens visited us. Mr. and Mrs. Allen had heard about the reason behind the fight between their daughter and Shireen. They had brought Gloria to apologize to Shireen. Mr. Allen who was in the army, assured Shireen that he thought of us as Americans, very good Americans, and that he didn't agree with Gloria's uncle at all. That night Shireen announced at the dining table, "I am going to be the best American from India. I'll be the best American in the whole world." That is when she demanded that we recite the Pledge of Allegiance every Friday but instead, my parents got a flag which was flown on our front lawn on her birthdays. Gloria and Shireen became good friends. They both became nurses and both went to Vietnam. Shireen met Max, married him and died in the service of her country.

Annie said, "Who wants to write such scripts anyway?" And then she told me why green Jello with fruit cocktail was her most important comfort food. Her eyes remained deep black as she spoke.

"As you know," Annie said, "my mother died when I was five. She died a few weeks after Max was born. Max and I were brought up by our father and his sister, Aunt Mabel."

Annie didn't speak very often about her mother or her mother's death.

"During my mother's funeral, I heard one of the women say, 'Shouldn't someone inform Mr. and Mrs. Richardson about Ellie's mother's death?' 'No,' said Aunt Mabel, 'Part of the deal was that we would not have anything more to do with Ellie. And anyway she is only five years old.' I was trying to find anything that would help me move away from the pain of my mother's death. I said, 'I too am five years old!' And the woman who had spoken earlier said, 'Of course, dear, Ellie after all is your twin sister.' And that is when I found out that I had a twin sister who had been adopted out the day we were born.

"I went to my father and demanded that since he said he couldn't bring back my mother, at least he should bring back my sister. She wasn't dead and a sister would help me stop hurting so much inside my eyes, chest and stomach. All the places in me where, I told him, I missed my Mom the most. My father went to his bedroom, carried Max to me and put him in my arms and then walked out of the house.

"To this day, neither my father nor Aunt Mabel will tell me anything more about my twin sister's adoption. Except that they had promised that no one in the family would ever try to contact Ellie.

"That first time I heard about my twin sister, at my mother's funeral, I could not stop crying. And I wouldn't let anyone come near me. I sat down on the floor, holding Max, and I cried and cried. I let my father take Max when he promised me that no one would take Max away from us. But I refused to eat anything for nearly two days. When I saw my Aunt Mabel crying, I asked her if she were crying because of my mother and my twin sister, she said, 'No, I am crying because I don't know what to do to make you eat. What to do to make your pain go away.' And I said, 'OK, I'll eat. But something nice and special. Something sweet!' And since the US Government always provided us with lots of Jello and canned fruit cocktail, Aunt Mabel made me a big bowl of green Jello with fruit cocktail. She held me on her lap and fed me that whole bowl of Jello herself. And she sang me songs and told me stories and kissed me at least four times. As you know, Aunt Mabel is not into overt demonstrations of affection. I stopped crying and sometimes it seems as if I haven't stopped eating since that day! And green Jello with fruit cocktail always reminds me that I do have people who love me. And it nearly always comforts me. It didn't when we got the news about Shireen's disappearance."

"Death." I corrected her.

Does death make ancestors of us all? I didn't ask that question aloud. Annie asked it when my mother died eight months before Annie and I graduated from Berkeley. And she asked the question again when our friend Homai died in Chiapas soon after I had retired from Sierra College.

SARIS, SARAPES AND SKELETONS
Bones the Color of Bones

Homai Laura Salazar-Sethna, the only child of a Mexican American mother, a war photographer, and a Parsi father, a "naturalized" citizen of the United States of America, died somewhere in Chiapas in the early 1990's. Since Homai born in Los Angeles in the late 1920's was a citizen of the United States of America and had listed me as her next of kin, someone from the US Embassy in Mexico City called me to inform me about Homai's death.

Late that same afternoon, I found a letter from Homai in my mailbox. It was mailed from San Cristóbal de las Casas three weeks before her death.

Despite my mother's belief that all Parsis are related, Homai and I were not related. She had no living relatives. In Mexico, India or the United States of America. She decided to put me down as next of kin when she discovered that my mother had taught me to cook a number of dishes that were a blend of Texan, Mexican and Indian Parsi cuisine. Homai had been known to put down "ParsMexicana" in the slot allowed for "other" on forms that demand one's ethnicity. Questions about race elicited "race is a construct created through complete lack of knowledge regarding human genetic biology." That statement was, of course, abbreviated or lost in the short space allocated for the race-response.

Homai used her credentials as a poet, a journalist and a paramedic to travel. She marched with Martin Luther King. She went to North Vietnam. She went to Bhopal before Bhopal blew up and walked around town carrying a placard that said, "My father walked with Gandhiji on the Salt March. My father and

Gandhiji would not have allowed a nuclear plant in India."

Homai was prone to grand statements and impulsive actions.

Homai went to China before the USA allowed her citizens to visit China. She went to Tibet to protest China's presence there. She worked with César Chavez. She got involved with Green Peace activists. She chained herself to trees. She went to jail. She went on hunger strikes. She bore exquisitely carved scars from politically sanctioned, perfectly executed torture in Chile and Guatemala. She was aware that her government in subtle, ignoble ways had trained her torturers. And she died in Chiapas.

The man who called me from the US Embassy in Mexico City regarding Homai's death informed me that there was very little left of anyone's body after the bus Homai was riding had crashed and caught on fire. There was no physical body to hold in mourning, to bury, to burn.

I met Homai in the women's room in Dwinelle Hall at the University of California in Berkeley. Annie introduced me to Homai. She had met Homai during a political gathering in front of Sather gate. It was the year Annie and I graduated from Cal. We were walking through Dwinelle Hall on our way to a screening of a documentary on Nepal when we heard loud voices emerging from the women's bathroom at the end of a hallway. One of the voices was screaming, "Help! Help! There is a crazy lady in here!" We ran into the bathroom to see two women struggling with one another. The tall, thin woman had short white hair sticking out all around her head like a child's drawing of the sun with its rays popping out every which way. The other woman was much younger and wore an Indian skirt and a T-shirt with "Question Authority" printed on the front and "Mary Poppins Is a Junkie" on the back. When Annie went towards the two women to pull them apart she recognized the older woman and shouted "Homai! What are you up to?"

Neither of the women paid any attention to Annie. Both of them pushed her aside and continued struggling with one another until I threatened to call the police. The two women disengaged at once. They glared at me and said, "Don't you dare call the police." Actually, the older woman said "the cops;" the younger woman said "the pigs." The white haired woman smiled, grabbed my hand, shook it with terrifying vigor and said, "Hello! Are you Annie's friend, Rhoda? Thanks for bringing me to my senses. My name is Homai Laura Salazar-Sethna. Hello Annie." And then she grabbed the younger woman's hand and introduced herself again. The younger woman muttered that she was "Judy." Homai said, "I acted horribly. Please accept my apologies. Does your T-shirt mean that you are an authority on questions or that you put questions to people in authority?" The vigorous handshake on the part of the older woman dislodged the voluminous sleeves that covered her arms. That is when I saw some of the scars on her arms.

Annie ushered us out of the bathroom in Dwinelle and demanded an explanation from Homai for her attack on Judy.

Homai had lost her temper when she entered the bathroom and found Judy systematically trashing one of the stalls. Judy had brought garbage from her kitchen, added the garbage from the bins in the Dwinelle bathroom and was dumping all the garbage into the toilets. Things like trashing libraries and bathrooms happened in those days at Berkeley. It was considered an imaginative variation on the different ways of demonstrating one's anger and frustration against the government, against one's parents, against the war, against having to fill out endless forms. Homai couldn't understand how anyone would be so stupid as to think that destroying a bathroom would stop the war in Vietnam. She was furious on behalf of the janitors who would have to clean up the extra mess without any extra remuneration. She had grabbed the back of Judy's T-shirt and threatened to dunk her head in the same toilet bowl in which she had been stuffing all kinds of garbage. Judy had fought back and yelled for help. We had appeared on the scene, rescued Judy and after the introductions and her apology, Homai invited Judy, Annie and I for dinner.

Annie and I decided to forget the documentary on Nepal. In the Indian restaurant on Telegraph Avenue, Homai deplored the inclusion of celery into a perfectly good vegetable curry and tried to persuade Judy that her anger was not against Judy as a human being but against her actions. Judy said, "Lady, what I do is what I am." Homai talked about disciplined, loving action. Annie pointed out that she hadn't seen any disciplined, loving action on the part of Homai in that bathroom in Dwinelle Hall. Homai apologized once again. She walked Judy home because she didn't think the streets of Berkeley were always safe for young women. "Because," she said, "ninety-five percent of the male population in this town will seduce you to warm their beds and make coffee for them while they plan the revolution and leave you to straighten out their rooms."

Over the next few years I got news about Homai from Annie and I suppose Homai got news about me from Annie. Sometimes the three of us met for a meal in Pescadero or San Francisco or Berkeley or San Mateo.

Homai was visiting Annie when I called Annie the evening after the commencement incident at Sierra College. I had been a professor at Sierra College for five years.

"Guess what, Annie," I said into the phone, "I got thrown out of the faculty procession of the Sierra College Commencement this morning."

As Annie went off to lower the volume on the radio, I could hear her say, "Homai, pick up the extension. Rhoda's in some kind of trouble."

When she got back to the phone, she said, "What do you mean you got kicked out of the Commencement? For God's sake, you are a full-blown, tenured professor at that college?"

"Let her speak." Homai was on the extension.

"One of the Marshals in charge of the faculty procession demanded that I leave the procession because I was wearing a sari and a shawl."

Annie pointed out that I had worn one of my mother's saris and the special black shawl my mother had embroidered for me at all the Sierra College commencements I had participated in the previous four years and no one had complained.

The shawl had a history.

My mother who didn't like to sew or embroider had started to embroider a shawl for me the first day of my Ph.D. program. She had called it "in-honor-of-my-Rhodabeh's-becoming-a-hakim-doctor-of-mathematics-shawl." She died before I completed my studies and I inherited her saris, the half-embroidered shawl, a strawberry blonde wig, her friendship with a woman named Ushabehen and her longing for at least one more glimpse of Shireen. I explained the shawl to Homai.

The idea of inheriting a wig fascinated Homai but Annie wouldn't allow Homai to ask me questions about my mother's death. She knew that I found the idea of talking about my mother, her bone cancer and her painful death difficult. She wanted to return to the Commencement and the shawl. She interrupted Homai's questions with an abrupt, "I know all that, Rhoda. So you wore the sari and that shawl. As we know, you have done that the last four commencements at the college and no one complained. Why this year?"

"Because it isn't traditional western, as in European, academic regalia. Last year, a faculty member had covered her face and head with a big mask of a Disney cartoon character wearing a mortar board and two or three other faculty members wore serapes-made-for-tourists at commencement and because of that the word was sent out that we were to wear clothes suitable to the dignity of the occasion."

Homai and Annie were, as expected, incensed at the idea of my colleagues considering a sari and a shawl or a serape undignified. They demanded "a full description" of the event. I told them about my colleague, the faculty procession Marshal who stood at least six inches above me, and her pronouncement that I could be in the faculty procession only if I wore traditional clothes. I assured Homai that I had countered with the obvious statement that I was wearing traditional clothes. At which point my colleague, the Marshal, had said, "Clothes. I am talking about clothes. Correct academic regalia from the institution where you received your highest academic degree. Not costumes and masks."

Annie reminded me that when we walked in our Ph.D. commencement exercises at Berkeley, she and about ten other students were the only ones who wore traditional, western, UC Berkeley regalia. I wore a sari and the shawl my mother had been working on. I was hooded over the shawl. Nearly everyone else was in the type of clothes one sees at Mardi Gras or a circus.

It had been quite a graduation. Even for Berkeley. Most of us were protesting the war in Vietnam with peace symbols appearing on various parts of our clothing or bodies. But the graduating students who had made the strongest impression on Annie and me were the ones who had worn macramé bikinis with walnut shell fringes under their academic robes. Every time they walked, the walnut shells swung across each other and made an awful 'clack-crack-clack-crack' sound. It drove the dogs on campus crazy. From Sather Gate to the different places of the numerous commencement exercises, the dogs of UC Berkeley followed those graduating students, barking and howling.

Homai didn't want to hear us reminiscing about our graduation, she wanted to know about my colleagues' reactions when I was told to leave their ranks. I told them that my colleagues standing around me had neither said nor done anything in support of me. The university band played the Academic Overture and my colleagues marched off. I returned to my office.

The silence on the other side of the telephone line wasn't very comforting. I tried to explain that I had felt stupid because I hadn't realized that my peers didn't consider me a colleague of theirs. "They most probably think of me as a freak because I don't always wear their kind of clothes and can never look like them. They don't think I am an American. They don't think I am human!" I stopped when I realized that I sounded like my sister Shireen saying, "I will prove to them that I am a real American" before she went off to Vietnam to die.

Annie was patient. "Rhodabeh," she said, "you don't quite understand this movie script. Most of your colleagues don't think the time has arrived to consider us as human beings. We are allowed to be super-human, perfect, either that or sub-human, civilization-destroying-monsters in disguise. Nothing more. Certainly not regular human beings."

"Stop pontificating." Homai wanted a solution.

Annie hadn't finished. "And even if you did wear garments ordained by them, what stops them from telling you next year that you can't walk with them because you do not have the right color of skin or because you weren't born here or whatever?"

And then she laughed. "Hey Rhoda, they are using you to pay for last year's Anglos in masks from Fantasia-land. Masks and serapes! They got away with that. It has happened at last! Your colleague revenged Custer's death at the hands of us Indians! One Indian to pay for the sins of the other Indians. Doesn't matter. This Indian. That Indian. But at last Custer has been honored on the campus of Sierra College."

I knew that Homai was struggling not to get into one of her sermons about "Us Indians from Asia are complicit in the continuing occupation of the Americas."

She shouted over the phone, "So, what are you going to

do about it, Rhoda?"

"Write letters, I suppose. Nothing. If I had insisted on walking in my sari and shawl, the police would have been called. What if they tried to disrobe me—people in the United States seem always to be interested in how a sari is worn."

"They wouldn't have dared! But they might have carried you off and out of sight."

"No god from no religion would have saved my honor. I am not Draupadi. I only wear one sari at a time and I do not even want to think of five husbands."

My effort at humor wasn't appreciated.

"Sue them." Said Annie. "Even with all your claims about not being a socially, politically active person, you have fought for civil rights, women's rights, and correct me if I am wrong, faculty rights. Now it is time to fight for your own rights. You are an American. Sue them. They won't like you if you sue them. But if you don't, they'll think that you are a wimp. And they'll treat you with even greater disrespect."

Annie had once threatened to punch a high school football coach who had refused to allow his team's name, Red Indian Warriors, to be changed. "What is all this fuss about?" He had asked. "The Red Indians lost many years ago. Get over it. We won. We can name our teams whatever we want."

Homai, of course, disagreed with Annie about a lawsuit. "What will that do? Who wants to spend money on lawyers! But first things first. We are coming over to your house. Right now. Come to Berkeley with us tonight."

And so they drove for nearly an hour and a half from Berkeley to reach my home on the Pacific coast, in Pescadero.

Before we left for Berkeley, we walked through the Pescadero marsh. Hawks, crows and seagulls rose from the marshlands and flew across the sand dunes lining Highway 1 and towards the Pacific Ocean. Homai composed a poem on the nunlike demeanor of an egret we saw standing in the marsh, snatching fish from the water and swallowing them whole. She named the egret Isadora Duncan.

Annie called a week later, when I was back in Pescadero, preparing for my annual summer visit to my father in Dallas.

"Rhoda, what have you decided to do about being kicked out of the procession?"

"Nothing. When I went back to the campus on the Monday after graduation, to hand over my grades, I found a letter of apology from the Chair of the Faculty Senate. I don't know that anything further can be done. I have to live with them, work with them, attend meetings with them. After all they are my colleagues. But I did receive one letter of support. From one colleague. The colleague I told you about. Her students call her the Zen Lady from Iowa."

"Who writes these scripts, anyway?" said Annie.

I didn't tell Annie that the colleague who had thrown me out of the procession had phoned me that same Monday. She hadn't apologized. "Hello Rhoda," she said. "Someone told me that you were quite upset last Friday. I asked you to leave the faculty procession because I thought you were one of those sarape types." At my, "I beg your pardon?" She said, "Oh you know. Like those men—fully tenured professors—who wore those silly sarapes last year at the Commencement instead of the correct academic regalia. Quite insulting."

When I asked, "Insulting to whom?" She muttered something that sounded like "You people are ridiculous."

I had silently screamed for Shireen, gone to the bathroom and thrown up the venom that had entered my body in the shape of my colleague's words and their silences. My mother had taught us not to swallow the poison other people injected into our lives. "Get rid of it," she would say, "I don't think we have reached Meerabai's exalted state. She could swallow the poison sent to her by the king and yet continue to live so that she could dance and sing in front of her Beloved. We will eventually sicken and die from the poison of those who disapprove of us." But our mother didn't tell us how we should to get rid of the venom. Anytime Shireen came home from a fight with her friends because of our looks, our accents, our names, the smells that emerged out of my mother's kitchen, my mother treated her physical wounds and gave her a laxative for the pain that Shireen said, "has made knots and pins and needles in my stomach." I had never fought back. I didn't know how to fight. Especially not fight women who were bigger than I and carried authority. They reminded me of the iron rigid Statue of Liberty. They reminded me of the stern, rigid statue of Queen Victoria we had been taken to look at when we stopped in London on our way to the United States. I always wondered if the British lady teacher who had slammed my mother's eight year old left hand in a drawer for speaking "Baboo English" and for denying Shakespeare's unique position looked like Queen Victoria.

A week after the phone call from the colleague who had dismissed me from the Commencement procession, Annie invited me to have lunch with her in Berkeley. After lunch, she drove me to a small house set among flowering mustard fields. Although the house was not far from Berkeley, it stood in complete isolation at the end of a long unpaved road.

The two women and the one man who lived in that house were physicians. They spent some time discussing ways Annie could help them raise money for medical care for abused children. And then they began to walk to a room at the back of the house. I followed them and heard Annie ask one of the women, "I received your call. About the child who was left in your office in the city. Still alive?"

"Might live." Said the woman. The room we entered had one small bed and a lot of medical equipment. On the bed was a child. I knew that the body on the bed was of a girl because Annie said, "Poor little girl. Wouldn't the hospital be better?" The child had been so badly beaten that some parts of her body did not have much skin left. There were burn marks on her face and arms and very little hair on her head. She was asleep.

"Yes," said the woman as she began to check the machines that were dripping fluids into the child. "A hospital would be perfect but not safe. We need to keep her hidden from her grandfather who beat her up, pulled out her hair, dragged her across his backyard and stubbed out cigarettes on her. He is bound and determined to kill her and will haunt every hospital in town until she is found and his work is completed. You can't write about where she is, Annie. He might read your article and find her here."

The physician then told us that the little girl had begged the doctors not to let her grandfather hurt her anymore. She had informed them that she was a bad girl because she didn't look like her grandfather or her father. She had said, "Their eyes are different. Their skin is so pretty. I have bad eyes. I am bad. I look like my mother and someone else. Not like my daddy. That's what grandfather said. He is ashamed to be seen with me. He is ashamed that my mother said that I was his family. He says that I have to disappear just like my Mummy and Daddy. I must not be seen. I am not his family."

We left the house soon afterwards and I drove off to Pescadero to pack for my annual summer trip to Dallas.

Homai sent me a postcard while I was in Dallas. It had a picture of a ceramic skeleton wearing an academic gown; a mortarboard was placed on top of the skull and a scholarly looking scroll was clutched tightly within the bleached bones of its right hand. The skeleton sculpture was created for a Día de los Muertos celebration in Oaxaca. Homai had written, "Let us have three cheers for the academic dead and the academically dying" at the back of the postcard.

The semester after the sari-sarape incident, the Faculty Senate passed an official resolution. Faculty members who wished to walk in the Commencement Procession had to wear the academic regalia of the educational institution from where they had earned their highest degree. All other faculty members who wished to participate in the commencement exercises but weren't dressed in academic regalia could walk at the end of the procession and sit at the back of the area set aside for non-academic robed faculty. It was also resolved to print a statement in the future Commencement Program brochures justifying the ruling about the dress code. It was to be an explanation of how the decision was based on a tradition of American universities that went back to the learned medieval monks of Europe. Wearing the academic regalia, the academic version of the medieval monk's regalia, was—according to the statement—to honor those monks and to show our respect for them.

I did tell Annie and Homai about the Faculty Senate resolution and the statement about medieval monks.

Homai was stunned at first and then she laughed. "Like it or not, Rhodabeh, they are bound and determined to prove that in the United States of America, even heathen Asians like you have been turned into good, little European children. Post-Toastie colonials. That's us."

Annie said, "You come from a tradition of universities that goes way before the medieval monks in their medieval universities in Europe."

Annie's mention of medieval monks set Homai off into laughter again. "Most of you on the faculty would have been excommunicated, damned to hellfire and sent to the stake by those good, learned monks. For reasons of religion, lack of religion, gender, sexual identity, women wearing men's clothes and men wearing God knows what under their correct regalia."

I spent the next six years at Sierra College learning that

Annie's words were true. I should have sued. That might have proved that I was a real American. When one of my colleagues visited my office and wondered aloud about how, Ratna Sharma, a professor who was born in Kenya could presume to present a proposal for a comparative literature department, I decided to retire. My body couldn't afford to keep on trying to get rid of other people's efforts to inject their insanity and disappointments into me.

Some years later, Homai announced that she was going to Chiapas. She invited Annie and me to go to Chiapas with her. I didn't think that an apolitical, ex-professor of mathematics could be of any help in Chiapas in the midst of a revolution. But I did go for a few months, learned about medical care in the midst of a war and then returned to Pescadero to participate in the Coastal Project Read Program. Annie spent a few more months in Chiapas and wrote a series of articles about her experiences there.

Homai remained in Chiapas and she died there. No one will ever know if the bus wreck was related to the war in Chiapas or if it was just a stupid, run-of-the-mill accident. It could have been a sharp curve, a careless driver that forced the bus off the road and caused the death of everyone in it.

That last letter which I received from her a few hours after the US Embassy had informed me of her death, was wrapped around a piece of white cardboard that looked as if it had been cut out from the top of a shoebox. It was about twelve inches by about six inches. Two photographs were stuck on it. The photograph on the right was of two elderly European Jewish men with long hair and beards walking on a road. They were wearing simple black robes and tall, square black hats. Three young men were circling them. They were in army uniforms with lots of leather. If you looked long enough at the picture you could smell the starch in their shirts and hear the squeaking of their brilliant leather boots. The pomade that kept the young men's short-cropped hair in perfect form glistened in the sunlight. Everything was in its correct place except for their bodies and faces. One young man was bent over, doubled with laughter as he pointed and jeered at the two old men. Another young man was in the process of spitting at them. The third young man was closer to his prey. He was grabbing the back of one of the elderly men's robes. He was intent on stripping the man of his robe. The two old men were looking straight ahead. Their faces calm, emotionless. In their eyes there was a desperate hope that all this was a nightmare from which they would be rescued.

The photograph on the left was of a funeral. The texture of tears and the sounds of grief were captured in the eyes and the hands of the people in it. Women, men and children surrounded the tiny coffins laid next to one another in the crowded small church. If there was even a glimpse of hope in that photograph, I couldn't see it.

Homai's letter reflected her disdain for traditional punctuation:

"Dear Rhodabeh—I am sorry I haven't written to you for a long time. . .I know, I know, in one whole year! No excuses. But, writing letters takes the lowest priority in my life right now. . .Thank you for your letters and "care" packages. . .I may not have received all of them but that is alright. Someone else got them.

"I am writing to you because I dreamed of you last night. You—Rhodabeh—appeared in my dream of an incident that took place three years ago. It happened a few months after I arrived here. Before you and Annie joined me. I knew the dream was a sign that I should write to you.

"The incident. . .not the dream. . .occurred here, in Chiapas. At a small, temporary hospital set up by the church. It was evening and quite a few casualties had been brought in. . .I was listening to two doctors trying to talk a young man into letting them amputate his left leg—he would have died otherwise—there were seven wounded and three dying men in that room. A woman walked into the room—said quite calmly, "Where are they?" The doctors and I just stood there looking at her—not understanding her question. "My two sons," she said. "I was told they are dying." I took her to the three men who were supposedly dying. She pointed at two of them and said, "They are dead." Actually all three men were dead when they were brought in but we were trying not to accept that. We were trying to save the man with the half-dangling leg. The woman dragged one of her dead sons out of the room and into the front courtyard. One of the doctors and I rushed towards her. To help her? To restrain her? I am not quite sure. She gestured towards her other dead son and asked us to bring him outside and lay him next to his brother. She then proceeded to strip both of her sons naked. One dead man was in a military uniform and the other dead man was in campesino clothes. Yes, he did have on a ski mask. But it was mostly torn off together with a part of his face.

"When the woman had stripped both of her sons naked, she said, 'Now they are as they came out of me. No clothes, no arguments. No land, no government to divide them. This one here,' she pointed at one of the dead men, 'thought the army would feed us and save us. And that one,' she pointed at the second man, 'went with the others. Now they are both dead.' She was absolutely sure that her two sons had killed one another. I told her a lie. I told her that the two men had been found in different places. She looked at me as if I were an idiot. 'What does it matter? If they didn't kill one another, they killed men and women who came out of some woman's body. And now both are dead.' She let us bury the men but she took their torn bloodied clothes with her and burned them in front of her house.

"Last night, in my dream, I saw the woman burning her sons' clothes. The woman was YOU. . .with your two dead sons lying on the ground in front of you. You pointed at them and I saw that not only were they naked, they had very little skin left on them. Their bodies were flayed as if they had been dragged across miles and miles of sand and rocks. I woke up crying and then I remembered that I had torn a picture for you from a magazine I had bought at the Mexico City airport three years ago. I wanted to read something while I traveled by bus from Mexico City to Oaxaca to San Cristóbal. That journey was a century ago! I have the picture stuck somewhere in my notebook. I'll give it to you when I see you. And we will laugh together. It is a picture of a little boy. About three? Four? He is wearing an academic robe and a mortarboard and is waving a rolled up diploma in his chubby hand. Of course, I thought of you when I saw the picture and so I tore if out for you. The caption says, 'Congratulations! Your baby has now graduated to real food.' It's an ad for cooked, bottled baby food. Mashed up vegetables, fruits, meats. . .what have you. So Rhodabeh, what do you think? Mother's milk isn't real?!

"I have always wanted to give you the two enclosed photographs. After last night's dream, it seems like the right time to do so. My mother gave them to me—her gift to me—when I graduated. She took the photograph of the men in Germany. Before the "official" war had supposedly begun in Europe. She took the funeral photograph years later in Mississippi.

"I have to go now and sleep for a few hours. I will be seeing you soon. I miss you. Are the pelicans back on Pescadero Beach? How can they be so ridiculous and so beautiful at the same time? Con prem y cariño. With all the love my father and my mother gave me, Homai."

I turned over the cardboard with the photographs and saw Homai's mother's spidery handwriting. "For my beloved daughter Homai Laura. There is neither an old world nor a new world. It is just a world. Con cariño, your mother, Ruth Laura Salazar de Sethna."

Homai has filled in the rest of the space on that cardboard with one of her rambling poems. It ends with the following lines:

My mother's eyes
camera lens
extensions
intercepting light
Clytaemnestra's web of vengeance
For sacrificed daughters and sons
ashes of the murdered
images
floating through film
the cells of her body
recording
our deaths
the frozen cruelty of
rape by words
murder by silence.

Jasmines and Grated Coconuts
Shadows of Songs and Flowers

My mother didn't write poetry or take pictures but she did leave me three legacies worth talking about. The black shawl she had embroidered for me as a Ph.D. graduation present, a long-haired, blonde wig she bought herself when the wretched chemicals that were to cure her killed her hair and she left me her friendship with Ushabehen. A friendship that began in Texas and was nourished in Texas. Although Homai and Annie had heard about Ushabehen, neither of them met her. They were not in California during Ushabehen's single visit to me in Pescadero. Homai was dead in Chiapas and Annie was visiting her Aunt Mable in Alaska.

We never did know Ushabehen's real family name. She used different last names at different times. We knew her as Ushabehen Mehta, Ushabehen Sethi, Ushabehen Mazumdar. At one time she announced that she was Ushabehen Ramirez and at another time she was Ushabehen King. Shireen and I used to call her Ushabehen-Jazmeen Soap Warrior because of our first impression of her.

It was on a Friday afternoon in June. I was thirteen years old and Shireen was about to turn eleven. She was engaged as usual in some perspiration-encouraging activity. Bicycling around and around the block or merely running through every neighbor's backyard, screaming at the top of her voice. I think it was the latter because I heard Mrs. Murphy, our neighbor to the left of us, shouting, "Shireen, stop screaming like a banshee. It is time you learned to act like a lady." It most probably was not very ladylike of the usually ladylike Mrs. Murphy to be yelling at Shireen but my sister was known to inspire people to deviate from their usual behavior patterns. I was putting together the jigsaw puzzle pieces of "The Great Prairie" on our kitchen table. Just as I was about to finish the wide-open, blue sky with of course, the smallest, most awkward piece of the puzzle, my mother walked into the room and announced that it was time for her to take us for our annual check-up at Dr. Simon's office.

Three minutes after the nurse had taken Shireen into the examination room, we heard Shireen wailing, "Mamma! Mamma!" Mother ran to the room and I followed her.

Shireen was sitting on the examination table and crying, "She's horrible! I am not—Mamma, I am not—" She was also trying to attack the nurse with her fists and her feet. Shireen was good at such things. I usually ran away from her whenever she began to fight. Doctor Simon had also rushed into the room. Shireen was still screaming and attempting to kick the nurse. We discovered that she was unhappy and enraged because the nurse had said, "You awful child, you stink." Doctor Simon said, "No, no Miss Johnson. It's just honest sweat. Shireen likes to run a lot and she also climbs trees." "No, it's not that." Said Nurse Johnson. "This child has that peculiar smell. These people always have this awful smell. They are dirty. Damn them."

A woman in a pink polyester pant suit and a bindi on her forehead wandered into the examination room just in time to hear Nurse Johnson's pronouncement. A strong smell of jasmines had entered the room with her. The woman rushed to the sink in the corner of the room, grabbed the anti-septic soap from the sink, ran water over the soap, went to Nurse Johnson and began to rub the wet soap across her mouth. "Bad words. Bad words. Wrong. Wrong!" Shouted the woman. Nurse Johnson tried to move away from the woman while yelling, "Get out. Your appointment is not till half an hour from now. How dare you come into this room!" My mother moved in between Nurse Johnson and the woman and quietly took the soap away. The woman then turned to Dr. Simon and said. "This is what my son Ramesh's teacher told me to do to him when he uses bad language. She told me to wash out his mouth with soap."

And that is how we met Ushabehen and that is when Ushabehen became my mother's dearest friend.

We knew nothing about Ushabehen's past history in India and very little about what had happened to her in America before we met her. And I cannot tell you what she looked like. But I can tell you about the sound and the smell of her.

The smell of jasmines was Ushabehen's olfactory shadow. Sometimes it was a soft perfume. Just a gentle smell of early mornings and babies right after their baths. And sometimes it was an overwhelming, stick-to-your-nose, sweet smell. The odor of life gone wrong, flowers in decay. Jasmines in full, quiet bloom or wilted, rotting jasmines were Ushabehen's shadow.

And no one could ever forget Ushabehen's voice. It was loud, deep and raw. Ushabehen usually turned her complaints and anger into laughter. Laughter that often made us uneasy. And even as children, Shireen and I heard fragments of pain and wounded bewilderment in Ushabehen's voice. Shireen once said to me, "Rhoda, something awful must have happened to Ushabehen. Her voice sometimes sounds like dry flakes of grated coconut. Without sugar. All shredded up."

When we were young, Shireen and I were prone to embarrassment regarding our Indian-accented elders. But we were never embarrassed by Ushabehen. Not even when she hummed, she muttered, she sang loudly and defiantly her unique rendition of the one line of the one song she knew, "Jaraa hatke, jaraa fatke yeh he Mumbai meri jaan." We weren't embarrassed even when she rendered the Hindi into her English version of "With a moving here and a pushing there, THIS, my dear, is MUMBAI-BOMBAY!" She repeated this line constantly. In her home, in our home, at the drug store where she worked, in restaurants, in shops, while waiting for buses and even while walking down our usually sedate streets. In order to make our mother laugh, Ushabehen would sometimes vary the line. She would drop Mumbai and would sing, "yeh he Dallas" or "yeh he Texas" or "yeh he Remember the Aalaamo-faalaamo" or "yeh he Mickey Mouse" or "yeh he very good sized prawns" or "yeh he complete madness-fadness, my dear."

It was again a Friday afternoon in June, many years after the soap incident, when we were informed that Shireen had died in Vietnam. Ushabehen came to visit us. She stayed at our home with my mother for forty days and forty nights. Her voice and the smell of jasmines comforted us. She agreed with my mother that since Shireen's body had not been sent to us, Shireen was not dead. She was just wounded and lost. Somewhere in Asia. The two women refused to mourn. They were holding a vigil to help my sister find her way back home. And yes, Ushabehen did sing about our Shireen. In the present tense, "Yeh he hamari Shireen, meri jaan" as she helped my mother around the house. And my mother sang along with her. The cracks in her voice widening as the days went on without us hearing anything further about Shireen.

My father did not, could not speak for nearly two weeks.

My mother wondered if we should fly a Missing in Action flag in front of our house. My father shook his head. Those sad, endless days when he would not speak, did not attend to his patients, he walked around the house and the back yard clutching the three pages with the words in Gujarati together with their English transliteration and translations of what he used to call, "the two brief but crucial Zoroastrian prayers" Ashem Vohu and Yatha Ahu Vairyo.

Shireen had insisted that my mother Xerox the pages for her from the large blue and gold Khordeh Avesta that had been given to our parents as a wedding gift by my mother's uncle. It was from this copy of the prayer book that my mother had taught us the prayers for our Navjote. Our father had insisted that we also memorize the translations. Shireen had decided to learn all the Kusti prayers and their translations as a special challenge. She had confessed to me that when she recited the prayers in the ancient language, she said "our sacred language," she felt that she would carry the ideas of virtue and purity and compassion from Iran through India to America. The prayers somehow became a part of her obsession regarding being "a Real and a GOOD American."

My mother had tried to pack the Xeroxed pages of the two prayers in Shireen's bag when she left for her training but Shireen had said, "Keep the pages, Mamma. I know the prayers and the translations. They are written in my mind. I will always remember them. Maybe I will frame the pages when I return from the war."

When Shireen told my mother to keep those pages, Ushabehen was with us. She had come to bless Shireen before she left. Ushabehen had hugged my sister and said that she would give her a special bottle of jasmine perfume when she returned home. Ushabehen was crying not only because Shireen was leaving but also because her own son, Ramesh had received his draft notice a few days earlier.

Ramesh was in the Air Force. Ramesh had also wanted to prove that he was the best American from India that one could ever be.

Eight months after we received the news about Shireen's death, Ramesh's body was mailed back to the United States in the requisite box, covered with the requisite flag. My mother went to stay with Ushabehen for forty days and forty nights. The two women sang bhajans at dawn and at twilight. I didn't hear Ushabehen singing anything about her son. No hatke-fatke and nothing about Mumbai.

In his last letter to Ushabehen, Ramesh had informed her that he had fathered a son in Vietnam and that he was planning to bring him to America at the end of the war.

On the forty-first day after Ramesh's body had arrived in

the United States, Ushabehen said to my mother, "You need to go and bring Ramesh's son to America."

"Why me? You should go, Ushabehen. I'll help you to go to Vietnam to bring your grandchild back here."

"Can't." Said Ushabehen.

"Why can't you?" Asked my mother.

"Because if I leave, I can't come back."

"Why?"

"Because I have no papers. Not to be here and not to be where I came from."

"I'll get you papers. For America." My mother could take things in her stride. And she was resourceful.

"I don't want any papers. I just want my grandchild. You go. Find my grandchild. Look for Shireen. Bring them both back. You know all these government things. You have worked for the Red Cross for many years, meri jaan. You have papers saying you are an American. You go."

And so my mother went to Southeast Asia and came back with a girl about six years old named Tara.

Ushabehen was somewhat surprised at getting a granddaughter instead of a grandson but my mother's explanation satisfied her.

According to my mother, she was unable to find Ramesh's son in Vietnam. The United States Air Force wouldn't help her. It had more important things on its mind. The war wasn't going well. Which, as she said, wasn't too surprising since wars seldom go well. So my mother went to Cambodia because she thought she would find Shireen there. She had dreamed of Shireen against the ruins of Ankor Wat. Instead of Shireen, she found a little girl hiding in the forest on the edge of one of the minor ruins. The girl followed mother to the cycle rickshaw my mother had hired, got into the rickshaw and told the man who drove the rickshaw to take her to her grandmother. My mother and the rickshaw driver who turned out to be a student of Sanskrit, spent three weeks looking for a grandmother who would claim the little girl. When no such grandmother was found by either of them, the rickshaw driver persuaded my mother that the girl should be taken back to America. He told her that the little girl was my mother's daughter reborn. When I heard this explanation, I told my mother and Ushabehen that although I was the only functioning mathematician among us, even a non-mathematician could figure out that Ramesh had certainly and definitely not been in Asia when the young girl Tara was born and anyway we all knew that if Shireen were to be reborn, she would not be reborn in Asia. She preferred the USA. My mother told me what she told the rickshaw driver, "You have to be dead before you can be reborn. Shireen is not dead."

My father continued to stay away from any argument or discussion about Shireen.

No one ever dared to ask my mother about how she had been able to take a child out of Cambodia and bring her into the United States of America. My mother was a resourceful woman. And she was also as rationally awe-inspiringly and inflexibly persuasive as the women she told stories about to Shireen and me when we were children. I always thought of my mother as Draupadi, Savitri and Sita combined. I suspect she used the Red Cross, various adoption agencies and maybe even Canada to smuggle Tara into the United States of America. And then a few years later, she somehow managed to get Tara genuine, legal American citizenship.

After my mother's death, Tara began to talk about the strange sounds she heard every night and the terrible nightmares that haunted her right into the middle of the day when she would abruptly fall asleep in the middle of her classes. Sounds and dreams from the first years of her life when she had wandered around looking for her grandmother. Ushabehen tried to dispel them with her love and with teas and herbs and medications and chants and prayers. But the sounds and the nightmares persisted.

When she was about twelve years old, Tara came all the way from Texas to spend a few days with me at my house in Pescadero. It was early January. We went to walk on the beach one evening to see if we could sight at least one migrating whale on the horizon. Tara had announced that morning that she had heard the whales singing all night long as they traveled within a few miles from my house. Across the broccoli, brussel sprouts, pumpkin and flower growing fields, across the freeway continuously threatened by sand dunes, across the marsh, the beach and the rocks, Tara had heard the whales from within the ocean at midnight. We saw no whales, observed no sudden spouts of water in the distance. We ended up watching pelicans diving into the Pacific Ocean for their evening meal. Tara returned to Texas carrying two boxes of Mrs. See's assorted chews and nuts chocolates for Ushabehen.

She was in middle school when she chose to deal with her nightmares with drugs. Ushabehen took her to doctors and counselors and hospitals and half-way houses and treatment centers but no one could help her.

One day, when Tara was still in school, Ushabehen phoned me to tell me that she was coming to California. "At last, I will see California meri jaan" she said.

I picked her up at the San Francisco airport and drove us to a restaurant near Pescadero which specialized in vegetarian food. The shadow of a slowly circling buzzard appeared and disappeared, etched dark against the dried grass of the hills next to the restaurant. Ushabehen looked at the menu and said, "yeh he healthy-felthy restaurant, meri jaan." While our waitress was taking our order, Ushabehen sang softly, "yeh waitress is a nakh-nu-ticchku, noseee is in the air, meri jaan." And that was true. The waitress was barely polite as she took our order. I was surprised that Ushabehen didn't sing about the elderly couple sitting at the table on our left. They weren't overly polite either. They were staring at us and quite obviously talking about us.

Ushabehen pulled out a map of North America from her bag, pushed aside the dried flower arrangement from the middle of our table and spread the map between us. As she leaned over the map I could smell a trace of her jasmine perfume.

"Ushabehen, can I please have a bottle of the jasmine perfume you make?" I asked.

"This is no time for perfume talk, Rhodabeh. Tara has disappeared. I have to find her." And Ushabehen started tracing the line of demarcation between the United States of America and the United States of Mexico.

"It goes bumping up and down. Who made it?"

"What?"

"This line. It looks more like holes in a sieve joined together."

"Where is Tara, Ushabehen?"

Ushabehen said, "I want your mother's hair."

I didn't know what she was talking about. So she raised that good, strong, grated voice of hers and repeated her request in Gujarati, "Mane tara Mamma na baal joiyech."

The older couple on our left nearly jumped out of their chairs. The waitress came briskly towards us.

Ushabehen didn't pay attention to anything that was going on. She raised her voice a bit louder. "I want your mother's wig. Her blonde w-e-e-e-g, Rhodabeh, meri jaan."

By now the waitress had reached us. "Ma'am," she said. "Please lower your voice. You are disturbing the other customers."

Ushabehen raised her voice even louder, "Jaraa hatke, jaraa fatke, this is a very rude waitress, we won't tip her, meri jaan."

At this point the waitress said something that sounded suspiciously like, "Oh shit. A drunk!" She tried to move Ushabehen's chair, with Ushabehen in it. Ushabehen began to laugh and demanded soap to wash out the young woman's mouth. I jumped up to stop the waitress from unseating Ushabehen but the older couple that had been staring at us had already reached her. The woman was trying to get the waitress away from Ushabehen by pulling on the waitress's pony-tail. The man was helping Ushabehen rise from the chair. The waitress was yelling at the manager to call the police. I was adding to the confusion by demanding our bill. Ushabehen was continuing to sing about the waitress. The four other customers who were in the restaurant were watching us, trying to decide if they should interfere in what most probably looked like a cross between an interracial sit-com and the Twilight Zone. With two brown aliens at the center of the action. Not always the most comfortable position to find one's self in when members of the SanDiV gang, the San Diego Vigilantes as Annie called them, roamed at will throughout California and could be checking up on us anytime, anywhere. Even in vegetarian restaurants. Even on a fogless, serene autumn afternoon of buzzards and red-tailed hawks on the Northern California coast.

As the restaurant manager began to walk towards us, the old gentleman who had persuaded his wife to let go of the waitress's hair, led his wife, Ushabehen and me out of the restaurant and into the parking lot.

"We heard you talking. Gujarati." He said.

"My husband and I were in India. We followed Gandhiji for a year. He was a great man. We learned a little bit of Hindi and a little bit of Gujarati." Said the woman.

"You followed Gandhiji in India and pulled that poor woman's hair in California!" Ushabehen was laughing.

And then she began to cry. Without any sound. There were no sobs. No trying to catch a breath. There were just tears.

After a few seconds, she blew her nose and said, "All I was trying to do is ask Rhodabeh for her mother's wig."

"Of course you can have it. But why?"

"Because Tara is gone. One of her friends came to my house yesterday to tell me that Tara was trying to get away from the drugs and she told the police about the bald man who sold drugs to her friends—just as I told her to do if the man came near her again—and the man got very angry and told her he would kill both of us. Tara and me. Tara got very scared and instead of coming to me, she ran away. She told her friend that if she went to Mexico, the man would think she was dead and then he wouldn't hurt me. I have to go to Mexico and I have no papers and I want to disguise myself and go. . ."

"Won't work." Said the man who had introduced himself as John Gregory and his wife as Joy Gregory.

"Yes, it will. You always forget that once upon a time, I was a Hollywood starlet." Said Joy Gregory. "Follow us in your car. We live only a few miles from here."

As we followed them to their house, I remonstrated at this rather unexpected and definitely dangerous course of action. Ushabehen told me to stop worrying.

Joy Gregory showed Ushabehen how to apply make-up. First there were layers upon layers of flesh-toned foundation creams. Creams of different flesh-tones that started with what looked like beige and ended up with a final cover of what looked like a mask made of melted-together tutti-frutti ice-cream. A blend of milk chocolate brown, Mylanta white and synthetic strawberry pink. A mask that might possibly fool someone into thinking that Ushabehen was attempting to cover a natural tan with what could be a basic pink and white make-up job. All this went onto Ushabehen's hands and face. Then there was a bit of lipstick, a bit of rouge, a bit of eye shadow on the face. While Joy was working on her, Ushabehen told her about my mother and Shireen and

Ramesh and Tara and she memorized the make-up process. Loudly. Like a child memorizing her multiplication tables. When she was finished with the make-up, Joy pulled out a pair of green non-prescription contact lenses and an auburn wig from a hat box. As she fitted the lenses and the wig onto Ushabehen, she explained that these were from her "Go as Lilith the Witch" Halloween ensemble. And then Joy gave Ushabehen her passport and told her, "From now until you find your granddaughter and bring her back, you are Joy Gregory going on a visit to Mexico. When anyone asks you for your papers, just show this passport. They'll think the woman in the photograph has dyed her hair and gotten new eye color in an attempt to look younger."

I thought the whole scheme was crazy and offered to go myself to find Tara. But Ushabehen refused. "No. This time I will go."

Before I took her to the airport, Ushabehen looked at herself in the mirror in my hallway and started laughing, "Look Rhodabeh. Jaraa hatke, jaraa fatke yeh he—this is a new Ushabehen-Joy meri jaan!"

She gave me a bottle of her jasmine perfume and she flew over that porous border.

Six days later, when I returned from a conference in Boston, I got a phone call from Joy. Ushabehen had been trying to reach me to tell me that she had been arrested in Mexico City but everything was fine now. She had been released and was on her way home.

"With or without Tara?" I asked

"With her granddaughter. The young woman was trying to beg in Mexico City, dressed up as one of those clowns. Performing for the motorists who stop at traffic lights."

I said I really didn't think Tara would ever dress up as a clown.

Joy assured me that she knew from her own experience

that one would dress up even as an earth-bound, winged insect if one had to for basic survival.

According to Joy, Ushabehen had found her granddaughter when a taxi driver told her of a fight between the regular performers-for-pesos and a foreigner. A young girl from China or from India, he said. When Ushabehen approached Tara, Tara tried to run away. In the ensuing chase Ushabehen lost her wig and her make-up started to crack and fell down her face and onto the ground in multicolored flakes. Even then, nothing would have happened if Tara had not fallen down and the police hadn't thought that Ushabehen was trying to kidnap Tara. The police arrested both of them. When they discovered that there had been no kidnap attempt and Tara was able to assure them that Ushabehen was her beloved grandmother, they released the two women.

Ushabehen told Joy that she would call me as soon as she reached the United States.

She called very late one evening. She said, "Rhoda, I am still in Mexico. Don't say anything. Just listen to me. I am calling from one of those public phone places and I don't have too much money left and I have to hurry. Tara and I are going to cross the border. Into California. That drug man followed her to Mexico and thinks we will come into Texas. I have to smuggle us back in. She ran off without any papers and since I lost all my make-up and all that stuff, I really can't use Joy's passport. They will arrest me for stealing her passport. And then they will deport me. Don't worry. After all, it's nothing. Jaraa hatke, jaraa fatke, just a few steps from here to there, meri jaan. I'll be in touch." And then she hung up.

But she did not keep in touch.

About a week and a half after Ushabehen's phone call, I got a call from a police officer. He wanted me to identify two bodies. A woman and a young girl. They had been shot somewhere near an isolated trailer park in the mountains around San Diego. The mountains that look as if a lunar landscape had been set on fire and burned brown before being dumped onto Southern California.

The police officer was vague about what had happened. He spoke about two strange women being seen wandering around the mountains, near the trailer park. There was also a man in the vicinity. The officer didn't know if the man was with the women or if he was following them. He wouldn't tell me much more. Joy and I found out later from newspaper accounts that when some of the trailer park dwellers sighted the three strangers, obviously trying to use their territory to enter into the United States of America, they decided it was time for action. About fifteen of the trailer park residents, women and men, got into five sturdy vehicles and tracked down the two women. The man eluded them. They pursued the two women with honking of horns and lights on high beams until they were able to pin them against the wall surrounding the trailer park. Someone called 911. The police and the man who had followed Tara from Dallas to Mexico to California arrived at the scene at the same time. There were conflicting reports as to who fired what and how many shots at whom. The two women and the man were killed. The older woman had twelve dollars, an American passport issued to Joy Gregory and a piece of paper with my name and phone number in the pocket of her pants. The younger woman was dressed in what looked like remnants of a clown costume.

Joy and I flew down to San Diego and drove to the morgue. I wish I could say that I smelled jasmines when the two faces were uncovered. I couldn't smell anything. And there wasn't even a memory of songs or of whales in the vicinity of the two bodies. When the man asked me, "Ma'am, can you identify these two women?" All I could say was, "No, I can't. How can I? There is such a God awful silence in here."

It was left to Joy Gregory to identify Ushabehen and Tara, to make their funeral arrangements and to tell me that it was time for me to go and search for my sister in Asia. But I didn't go to Asia. Not then.

Many years later when Annie and I returned from India, I asked Annie if a person not related by blood but by friendship could be one's ancestor.

The Man they Called Samson
Chakras Moving through the Blues

I could not see the man at my front door but I heard laughter and a hint of self-mockery in his voice as he introduced himself to Roxanne Japanwallah who had gone to answer the doorbell. "Good evening lady!" He said. "Don't worry. I am one of the good ones."

Roxanne Japanwallah, daughter of my mother's cousin twice-removed was Devinagar's most trusted lawyer, well-known amateur sleuth and dexterous manipulator of languages. When she had phoned me from the airport four days earlier, she was shouting as if it were a long distance call from India. "Rhodabeh! Hello! Hello! I am your cousin Roxanne Japanwallah. From Devinagar. In India, you know. I used to exchange letters with your mother— before she died— of course. In every letter she insisted that her daughter, your sister Shireen was still alive. I have just arrived from India and I wonder if I can stay with you in Pescadero-Fescadero. I am here to solve the mystery of your sister Shireen's disappearance."

My contribution to the phone conversation consisted of the initial "Hello. Of course. I will come to the airport to pick you up" and nothing else. Roxanne said, "Thank you, Rhodabeh," gave me her location at the airport and hung up.

Four evenings later, Roxanne was telling Annie and me that she was determined to use all her skills to find my sister— "dead-fed, alive-balive or in-between"— when my doorbell rang announcing the arrival of the man who claimed that he was one of the good ones. I had been repeating what I had been saying for the last four days to Roxanne and Annie. Shireen was dead. There was no mystery. If she were alive we would have found her by now or she would have made her way to us. She had inherited our mother's resourcefulness.

Roxanne had been shouting at me, "Rhodabeh Sohrabji, you are a mathematician. . .you should know that there are always mysteries-fisteries. . .there are always probabilities and possibilities. . ." when the doorbell rang. She was still talking about mysteries and mathematics when she got up to answer the doorbell.

When we heard the man's statement about being one of the good ones, Annie wondered what religion he was trying to sell. It was too late in the evening for a visit from the Jehovah's Witnesses. The local Baptists had given up on me after two visits.

We heard Roxanne asking the man. "What are you good at?"

His answer was, "Good evening. Would you like to subscribe to some magazines?"

"Don't know." Replied Roxanne.

The man said, "I like your earrings. Where are they from? India? We have travel magazines."

Roxanne was matter-of-fact. "Thank you. No, they are from China. How do you do? I am Roxanne Japanwallah from India. What are you good at?"

"Good at?" He asked.

"You said you were one of the good one. Fine. But what are you good at?"

"Oh that! That was to make you feel safe. But Roxie, I can call you Roxie, yes? I am good at many things. I can repair cars. . ."

The man, I am sure, was looking at my rather old red Mustang with envy and disgust. That car needed work. Parking it outside to be assaulted by the sea breezes from the Pacific Ocean had not been kind to it.

". . .and I am pretty handy around the house. I can even

cook. My Mama taught me well. And I can sing the Blues. Like no one can sing the Blues. No one now. . ."

"Blues? I would like to learn about the Blues." Said Roxanne. And then to Annie's and my amazement she said, "Come in. This is my cousin Rhodabeh Sohrabji's house. Most people call her Rhoda."

The young man Roxanne ushered into the living room was wearing a brown suit and tortoise shell glasses. We couldn't see his hair because it had been crammed with great determination under a brown woolen cap.

He shook hands with Annie and me, introduced himself as Grant Parsons and turned to Roxanne. He was on a mission. To teach his new friend from India the Blues.

"Let me tell you about the Blues, Roxie! First the music begins right from here. . ." He took Roxanne's hand and placed it somewhere near her diaphragm.

"From your guts. Your heart. Between your guts and your heart. The sound, it has to start there. And then Roxie, it begins to travel. . ."

Annie pointed to the piano in the kitchen. That is where I had placed the lime green piano I had found at a garage sale in Half Moon Bay. The old gentleman who sold me the piano had assured me that "Don't Sit under the Apple Tree with Anyone Else but Me" was composed on that particular piano. It was my father's favorite song. I had always supposed it was his favorite song. It was the only song I had heard him try to sing. Annie knew all the words to the song. I bought the piano for my father. Hoping my father would decide to live with me in Pescadero after he retired. According to my mother, my father was a very good pianist who had decided to give up the piano when he began his dental practice in Texas.

Grant Parsons looked at me. I nodded. He went to the piano, began to play and then he sang.

As that fog-bound evening turned into a cold, hard-edged autumn night, as the two barn owls flew low over the fields across from my house, as the wind arose and the cottonwood tree in my back yard rustled like a lady in a long taffeta skirt, we listened to Grant Parsons singing.

Annie and I tried not to make any noise. Roxanne laughed, she cried, she urged Grant to repeat lines with, "Wah! Wah! Bravo! Definitely Bravo!" It was a ritual of great joy and reverence between the middle-aged lady lawyer from India and the young man who defied anyone to forget that he was descended from men and women who had been royalty and slaves and factory workers and artists and healers and educators and bridge builders and lovers. Above all lovers, warriors, survivors with a visceral, intimate knowledge of the songs they sang, of the bodies that produced the songs, of the yearnings, the disappointments, the visions of joy and victory which ran like fine threads—gold and black—holding the songs together.

I don't know how long Grant Parsons sang and coaxed that silly green piano to sing along with him but at last he looked up and laughed.

"Roxie from India," he said, "Now you understand the Blues! My Mama says that the Blues are good for life, for what ails you. But not good for making a living. She says college is good for making a living. So instead of the Blues, I am peddling these magazines! Get subscribers for them, the publishers told me, and they'll send me to college. Imagine. Do you believe it?"

We invited Grant to stay for dinner.

Roxanne talked throughout the meal. She told Grant that the Blues he had sung were "Good chakra-cleansing music. From the third chakra in the middle of my body, it traveled down, all the way to the tip of my feet. Supposedly no chakras there according to some-who-are-in-the know. And then right up and off the top of my head. Just like Meerabai's bhajans." Grant said, "I know something about meditation and those religious songs and the chakra points in the body. But never quite thought of the Blues in that way. Interesting. Meerabai?"

Roxanne sang. And after every few lines, she translated. Meerabai rejoicing in her love. Dancing. The sound of bells on her ankles weaving through her yearning for a reunion with her lover, announcing her victory over death, over worldly powers attempting to poison lovers.

She stopped abruptly and said, "Yes, think about it. The Blues for the chakras. What will you study in college?"

"Chemistry." Answered Grant.

"Why chemistry?" asked Roxanne.

"Because I am good at such things."

"What else are you good at?" She had an agenda.

"I am good at getting around and finding things."

"Me too." Said Roxanne. "I am a very good detective. Want to be a detective-fetective?"

"Sure." said Grant.

"We are trying to find Rhodabeh's sister. The army says that she was killed or lost in Vietnam. But we don't believe them."

"Why?"

"Because her body was never shipped back. They said that her body was never found."

"That happens in wars, Roxie." Grant was gentle.

"Yes. Everything happens in wars. But I don't believe that Shireen is dead."

"Why?"

"Because Shireen's mother who is dead now and Annie here who is Shireen's sister-in-law have refused to believe that Shireen was killed in Vietnam."

"Then I am sure your sister is alive," said Grant to me.

I just shook my head. Who was I to engage in a debate with a lawyer and a singer of Blues?

"I am in America to find out about Shireen. I am going to start with the United States Army."

Grant was appalled. "The army is no place to start or end with anything. Leave it be for God's sake!"

Annie said, "Amen! About the army part. But I think we can find her. I know she is alive."

"I am not enamored of armies-barmies either," Roxanne assured him. "But where else should one start?"

"No. Leave that be, Roxie. They will know nothing. But maybe my Mama can tell us. She has the sight."

Roxanne nodded. I tried not to think about where all this was leading.

"Always better to ask a woman than to tangle with an army. I would love to meet your mother." That of course was Roxanne.

And that is how we ended up in Grant's mother's apartment in San Mateo two days later.

Mrs. Parsons was all steel. From her round, steel-rimmed glasses to her gray hair, to her unadorned clothing and to her no-nonsense shoes she was a portrait of a woman who could not be bent. But when she spoke, one heard rivers and oceans and streams. Water that could flow gently, slowly, or with terrible, sudden force, changing whole landscapes of life.

Annie, Roxanne and I stared at Grant.

Annie said, "Well! What a surprise."

It wasn't the 49er's jacket, the casual pants and the absence of tortoise shell glasses that we were staring at. We were staring at his hair. I wondered how he had been able to push all that luxuriant hair under that cap he had worn two days ago.

Roxanne said, "If I had hair this gorgeous, I would never wear a hat."

Mrs. Parsons took charge of the conversation. "Grant tells me that you are trying to find out if a young woman is dead or just missing. Tell me about her."

When Roxanne finished explaining all about my sister Shireen, the United States Army's message, the missing body and my mother's belief, Mrs. Parsons turned to me and said softly, "Have you ever thought that maybe she doesn't want to be found?"

"I don't think that is possible. Her husband—my brother—is waiting for her." Annie was sure of herself.

I didn't want to think about the possibility that my sister would not want to return to us. When we had received the news about Shireen's death my body could barely contain my grief. The thought of a deliberate abandonment by my sister went beyond that pain.

Mrs. Parson's didn't wait for a response. "Yes, your sister is alive. But it is not time yet for you to go in search of her. She is well and is near a temple in ruins. With walls decorated with men, women, monkeys. There are dancers and there are men with guns. And there are vines trying keep old walls from falling down."

"And the walls will come tumbling down." Roxanne sang out.

I looked at her for an explanation. She ignored me, turned to Grant and said, "Back to your hair, Grant. Why do you hide it? You certainly don't think that someone will take you for a modern-day Samson? Seducer of the women, destroyer of the temples of your enemies? Wish I had hair like yours. When I was eight years old, I was not allowed to dance in the front row of a dance recital because my hair would not ringlet. The teacher wanted us all to be little Shirley-Burly-Wurly Temples for the Devinagar kindergarten performance of 'Daisy, Daisy all for the Love of You!'" Roxanne decided to sing variations on the song. It was "Delilah, Delilah, All for the Love of You" and "Samson, Samson, All for the Love of You."

Annie and I were embarrassed and looked at Mrs.

Parsons. She was laughing until Grant said, "My uncle was called Samson."

"My brother's name was Jason. Not Samson. He was a good man." His mother reminded him.

"Yes a very good man but they called him Samson after that lady forced the two men to shave his head. Without shedding a drop of his blood."

"Leave it be, son. It was a long time ago."

"Not so long ago. I was nine years old. That is not all that many years ago. But I suppose it was better to have watched those men shave uncle's head rather than see them cut it off. That's what they wanted to do."

"Shaved off his hair!" Annie was the first to speak.

"Yes."

Our silence demanded an answer.

"Because he had dared to say to the lady's daughter that he loved her long beautiful brown hair. He said it was like a waterfall of leaves in the fall." Grant explained.

"My brother Jason loved poetry." Mrs. Parsons was shaking her head.

We waited for more details. It was Grant who began the story for us. "It all happened in a small country store. Not so far from Raleigh, Durham and all those fancy towns in North Carolina. They weren't fancy then. Not only did Uncle Jason, later called Samson by most of our neighbors, say all those sweet things to Laura May but Laura May smiled and said to my uncle that she liked his hair! All curly and strong. 'Alive,' she said, 'alive.' It was when she reached over to touch uncle's hair that her mother screamed and the two men chased my uncle all the way home. It was a good thing my uncle could run faster than they could. He reached our house about five minutes before the two men came stomping up that porch. It was enough time for Laura May's Mama to catch up with the two men."

"When those two men reached our house they were shouting that they were going to cut off his head, cut off his hands. . ." Mrs. Parsons stopped speaking for a moment and wrapped her arms around herself. "Little Grant and I were right there. There on our porch when Jason came running with the two men after him."

"Did they harm him?" Roxanne wanted to run off into the past to bring the two men to justice.

"No." Said Mrs. Parsons.

"Yes." Said Grant.

His mother looked at him and nodded in agreement before continuing the story.

"Laura May's mother was right behind the two men. She had a gun in her hand. She pushed her way between Jason and those men and told the men to shut up. She threatened to shoot them if they punished Jason in the ways they were promising to do. But she insisted that they shave off his hair.

"She pointed her gun at me and said, 'Ma'am, please get a razor. Bring it now. Before these men get other ideas.' There was nothing I could do. So I brought my husband's razor. She then just stood there pointing her gun at those two men and said, 'Shave his head. Shave it clean. But if you as much as nick his skin anywhere I will shoot you.' And so my little son and I stood by as the two men shaved my brother's hair. They didn't draw any blood but they sure spoke words to cut a man deep and sharp. They kept on saying, 'This is not one of the good ones. We better keep an eye on him. Watch him carefully. All the time.' When the men were finished the woman told them to leave. They did. And she went off behind them. Still pointing her gun at them. But we knew they would return. She had shamed them and their work wasn't finished. The story about the shaving spread throughout the town and people started calling my brother, Samson. He left home two days later. He never returned. Not even for our mother's funeral."

Roxanne began to sing again. She had barely started with "Blood on the leaves and blood at the root" when Grant stopped her. "Why Roxie-Foxie, you knew something about the Blues all along!" He said.

Roxanne smiled. "I thought I was singing Jazz. I have always wanted to sing like Billie Holiday and wear a gardenia behind my ear."

Grant wouldn't let her get away with that. "Yes, I suppose it is Jazz. But that Lady, I tell you Roxie, she painted Jazz in shades of blue!"

Shades of blue. And I heard my little sister Shireen, her seven-year-old voice saying, "Mamma, when you come to my school Christmas concert will you wear your blue sari with the sprinklies on it?" And the day after the Christmas concert Shireen crying. "My friend Gloria says that we aren't real Americans. We don't go to church. Pappa speaks funny English and you wear funny clothes. Gloria's uncle told her that the government will throw us all out of America. Will they throw us into the sea Mamma or will they send us away on an aero plane? Mamma please, please stop wearing saris." And I heard my little sister Shireen, her nine-year-old voice pitched high and loud as she sang about the "red, white and blue." When she belted out "land where our fathers died" our mother repeated that her father had died in India and Shireen said, "You'll see. I'll be the best American one can be. The best American who was born in India." And our mother laughed and said, "Arré, what an ambitious child." Our mother, whose last words to me were, "My daughter did not die before me. She is alive."

I looked at Mrs. Parsons who had assured me that my sister was alive. She said, "I never saw my brother Jason again after he left our house in North Carolina. He left behind all his poetry books. Never sent for them. Never wrote to us or called us. No word about him until the army told us that he had gone missing in Vietnam. No use waiting for him. He is gone. His beautiful hair shaved clean off his head."

I wondered if Roxanne Japanwallah from Devinagar who had an answer for everything could explain the mathematical probabilities and possibilities, the mysteries and the laments embedded within the fragmented, sharp-edged shades of America's Blues. And I thought of my sister Shireen. Shireen who loved the color blue. "Blue—it is such a deep, deep color," she told me once when we were walking home from school. "And so wide. Just like the sky. Blue is my favorite color but sometimes it makes me sad. I don't know why." I remembered Shireen as she cried silently in fear as she looked across the blue tablecloth at Judy's father telling us about heathens, Christianity and America. I looked at Grant Parsons. The blues and chakras. Grant's mother whose brother who had disappeared from her life. Roxanne's determination to solve the mystery of my sister's disappearance.

AMERICAN DHANSAK AND THE HOLY MAN OF OAXACA

The Yellow of Turmeric

Roxanne Japanwallah and I went to Mexico. Instead of music, blues and bhajans, we got involved with food. Not the reds and blacks of mole but the deep yellow of dhanksak. When my younger sister Shireen and I were growing up in Dallas, my mother cooked Parsi Tex-Mex food. My favorite was something she called "chili per eeda." Texas-style chili—onions, beans, meat, thick, spicy red sauce—topped by sunny-side-up fried eggs. My father's favorite Sunday morning breakfast, ekuri—eggs scrambled with onions, fresh green serrano chilies, tomatoes, cilantro—had evolved into a Parsi combination of huevos rancheros and huevos mexicanos. Crisp tortillas covered with Parsi ekuri garnished with salsa, slices of avocado and melted cheese. Mother quite often made her own tortillas. She had learned how to make tortillas from our neighbor Señora Rachel. They didn't use rolling pins or tortilla presses. They pulled the dough into small balls and patted them into flat perfect circles with their hands. When Señora Rachel wasn't with her, Mother sometimes used the slender rolling pin she had brought from India.

While they taught one another the secrets of their ancestral cuisines, mother and Señora Rachel discussed the relative merits of the flexibility of reincarnation versus a fixed heaven-or-hell. The latter being a concept made popular—or as my father would say, "heaven help us—heaven, hell, behest, dojhuk—invented by our Zoroastrian ancestors." The two women's judgment on what kind of after-death they preferred vacillated. Mother once told me that the judgment depended on the degree of spiciness of the food Señora Rachel and she were cooking. Reincarnation was favored when the food was especially spicy hot. My mother called it, "Hot, hot haldi-marchi, turmeric-chilies, red-yellow food! Who wouldn't return to earth to taste such food again?" But when my mother first tasted Señora Rachel's mole Oaxaqueña, the red one, she announced that she was already in paradise.

My mother loved mole. And she cooked mole the way her friend had taught her to cook it. She roasted tomatoes, added the mole paste—black or red—that Señora Rachel gave her, added chicken broth, stirred all of it together and brought it to boil. When she thought the sauce was cooked enough she added chicken. When she thought the sauce needed more "oomph" (her exact words), she would add more marcha ni bhookhi, very hot red chili powder and chopped up Baker's bitter chocolate. The mole paste came in small plastic containers and was always the La Soledad brand. Señora Rachel bought these from her old school teacher, Maestra Sofia who had opened a store in Colonia Jalatlaco in Oaxaca. The store was a no-name store, La Tienda Sin Nombre. My mother's friend made two visits a year to her birthplace to see her family and her teacher and she always came back with enough mole paste for at least six mole feasts a year for all of us.

It was many years later, long after my mother's death, that I learned how complicated and how long a process it is to cook real, not from a prepared paste, mole. The careful pounding and grinding of spices, nuts, raisins and seeds with different types of dried chilies, the mixing of these with rough, rich, dark Mexican chocolate grated from solid blocks, the adding of the tortilla pieces and then cooking all the ingredients in a sauce in a large earthenware pot over charcoal for a long time. Sometimes as long as two days with near constant stirring. If my mother thought that the La Soledad based mole took her to heaven, I wonder what ecstasies she would have experienced from the moles cooked from scratch!

My mother loved mole and Señora Rachel loved dhansak. The fried rice and rich, spicy lentils that may be the closest the Parsis have to an ethnic signifier within South Asian culinary traditions.

I learned how to make dhansak from Señora Rachel because I noticed that she was much more efficient about making the daal than my mother. My mother wasn't the best cooking instructor. She always tried to teach me about marriage and sex during cooking lessons. I wasn't overly interested in learning about either subject from her. Marriage seemed remote and sex was much more exciting when I heard about it from my sister Shireen and her friend, Twinkles. That was Shireen's friend's legal name. Twinkles Johnson.

When I came to California, I continued cook dhansak the way I was taught by Señora Rachel. When I tried to cook dhansak in Oaxaca, México for my cousin Roxanne Japanwallah and the man known in Oaxaca as el santo de la india, there was trouble.

A few days after our visit to Grant's mother, Roxanne demanded that I go with her to Oaxaca because she disclosed that she really had two reasons for her visit to America. She had come to America not only to unravel the mystery of Shireen's lost body but also because she had been hired by a family in Devinagar to find their son. The son had come to the States many years ago to become a jazz musician but within a year of becoming a naturalized citizen, he was drafted to go to Vietnam. At that point, he decided to become a wandering holy man and a yoga teacher and had disappeared from the United States of America. The last letter his family had received from him was from Oaxaca.

Roxanne wanted me to go with her because she was convinced that since I had grown up in Texas and was now living in California, I could speak Spanish and therefore could help her find the wandering son. I found out that besides being brilliant, eccentric and adventurous, my cousin was also tenacious. Saying "no" to her was impossible. When I explained that I would be useless because I had just enough Spanish not to go hungry in a Spanish speaking country, she said, "We will learn as we travel."

When Roxanne and I arrived in Oaxaca, I asked her, "How do we find this man?" She said, "Just ask for the Indian holy man." That led us into some misadventures for three entire days. We were sent all around the state of Oaxaca to see curanderos and santos but none of them were from India. I realized my mistake. No, not my mistake but the confusion arising from Columbus' supposed mistake. When I specified that we were searching for the holy man from India, el santo de la india and not an el santo indio, an indigenous to the Americas, indios holy man, I was told to go to a restaurant called El Restaurante Internacional in Colonia Jalatlaco at 2:30 pm. El santo de la india always ate his comida there at 2:30pm. 2:30 was given as más o menos.

We went to the restaurant and decided that the man with untrimmed hair, long beard and white robe, sitting under the picture of Lenin was the holy man we were looking for. The restaurant espoused Marxist slogans on its walls and served a simple, inexpensive comida. Mole was not part of the menu.

Roxanne sat down across from the man and after a few seconds, I sat down next to her. The man raised his eyebrows in surprise and waited for us to speak. He didn't seem at all concerned about two strange women joining him without his permission. Before Roxanne or I could say anything, he said, "Buenas tardes." Roxanne grinned and greeted him back. "Buenas tardes! Are you a Parsi holy person?" The man laughed and thought for a moment.

He said, "I don't know about holy. I wear this robe because it is comfortable. But I am a Parsi. And now and then I teach my version of yoga."

"Prove that you are a Parsi!" Said my cousin.

The man put his right hand on his chest. I thought he was

about to tear open the top part of his robe to show us that he was wearing the white, muslin sadrah next to his skin that would prove that he was truly a Parsi, a bona fide, genuinely initiated follower of our ancient Zoroastrian religion. I also had visions of Hanuman tearing open his chest to reveal Ram and Sita enshrined in his heart while Jesus Christ and Mary looked on as they presented to the world their own hearts, surrounded by a barbed wire of thorns. Santana's song would have made a great background. The man didn't tear open his chest. He didn't even tear open his robe. He just scratched himself, thought for a moment and laughed again. He then leaned towards me and whispered theatrically, "My name is Erach Wadia. Can you make dhansak? The rice part isn't important. Just the daal. I'll eat it with tortillas."

"That's him. You are the right man. I am Roxanne Japanwallah and I am going to take you back to Devinagar." Roxanne was pleased with herself.

I said, "My name is Rhoda Sohrabji. And if you can get me some meat or chicken, some allspice, cayenne, turmeric, some onions, garlic, tomatoes, green chilies, cilantro, carrots, potatoes, a can of vegetarian split-pea soup—preferably Campbell's vegetarian split pea soup. . ."

Roxanne exploded out of her chair. Every inch of her five foot one frame and every ounce of her 95 lbs. were horrified. She complained bitterly about the watering down of traditions— sacred and secular. Remembering my father's insistence on dhansak being served every Sunday, I think the dish hovers somewhere between sacred and reluctantly-secular for many of my fellow Parsis, including my cousin Roxanne. She went to the proprietor of the restaurant and asked him if he had an English-Spanish Dictionary. He did. Roxanne found the word for lentils and the spices she needed and offered to cook real dhansak for the restaurant the very next day. She said that she would use only one type of lentils instead of the three types of lentils required for authentic dhansak.

I tried to explain how Señora Rachel had taught me to make the daal with vegetarian split pea soup. Jazzed up with meat, different spices, onions, tomatoes, dried red chilies and a lot of turmeric.

As I spoke about Senora Rachel's belief in the nutritive and healing powers of turmeric, Roxanne looked at me with her huge sorrowful eyes and I could picture myself as one of her clients who was really and truly guilty of a terrible crime and who even the brilliant Roxanne Japanwallah couldn't save from being punished by the law.

Roxanne, Erach, Mauricio—the restaurant proprietor-cook-waiter and Colonia Jalatlaco resident Marxist—and I went off to the market at 5:30 am. Erach and I wandered around the market while Roxanne and Mauricio shopped. The Eagles were singing *Hotel California* on nearly every boom box in nearly every stall in the market.

We couldn't find turmeric. After nearly an hour of searching for it, Roxanne and Erach trying to describe it, pointing to every yellow thing around them, Roxanne reluctantly allowed that she could do without it. Many years later, I was told that we should have asked for cumcumura. But during that first visit to Mexico, I didn't know the Spanish name for most of the spices. Señora Rachel had used the English names for the spices when she cooked in our kitchen.

At about 8:30 a.m., we went back to the restaurant where Roxanne cooked the daal with great flair and expertise. She refused to let any of us help her. As I watched her soaking the lentils before cooking them and later mashing and forcing the cooked lentils through a chipped, blue enameled colander, I remembered how long it used to take my mother to cook dhansak and why Señora Rachel had opted for canned vegetarian split pea soup.

Dhansak with meat, lentejas de la india con carne, was the main and only dish served that afternoon in El Restaurante International. Roxanne had cooked fried rice to go with the daal but most of the customers preferred to eat it with tortillas.

While Erach and I ate, Roxanne told us the story about her childhood neighbors, Jehangir and Alamai Patel and the dhansak lunch commemorating Jehangirji's death. According to Roxanne, Mr. Jehangirji Patel had died on Roxanne's thirteenth birthday just to spite her. Her birthday party was cancelled. Jehangirji was nearly ninety-four years old.

"My sister Gulnar and I didn't like Jehangirji." Roxanne had her reasons. "He always shouted at us and told my parents that I was a willful girl, which boded terrible things for my family. But Gulnar and I were very fond of his wife, Alamai. She was a terrific cook and she and our Grandmother Meheramai loved to go to the Great Empire Cinema Theater to see films. Alamai didn't care if they were Indian films, British films or American films. 'Pictures' she called them and approved of them only if they were filled with dances and songs. Her husband disapproved of her love of films and her attempts to teach us the songs and dances she had seen on the screen.

"Jehangirji walked into our house one afternoon as Alamai was teaching Grandmother Meheramai, my sister and me the correct way to look sexy and slink around our verandah while dancing the tango. He announced that Alamai was disgracing him. Going to the cinema was an evil habit and therefore no more cinemas for her. He told her that if she dared to disobey him, she would go to dojhuk, right down to hell and demons would pull her apart, limb from limb, as punishment for all the unnatural contortions she was learning from the films she saw. Alamai continued to go to the Great Empire Cinema Theater and to teach us the dances she saw on the silver screen.

"When Jehangirji died many years later, Alamai invited

us, my grandparents, my parents, my sister and me for the special fourth-day-after-the-funeral, breaking-the-meat-fast meal. Alamai had made the traditional dhansak. With chicken instead of mutton. She dished out the daal on top of our rice and as she selected a piece of chicken from the daal for each of us, she chanted, 'And this, dear friends, this dear children, is Jehangirji's right leg, and now this is his back—the left side, this is one of his thighs, this is part of his chest. Roxanne dear, bring your plate a bit closer so that I can give you one of his wings. A wing and a leg. He is now limb from limb and will fly off to paradise with our blessed, angelic Farohars to live with Ahura Mazda.' It was the most memorable meal I have ever had."

Roxanne finished her story and served more dhansak to everyone in the restaurant.

Erach said, "What a great lady she must have been! She knew about transcending threats, the transformation of souls and the dismemberment of bodies. And she could dance!"

Roxanne said, "She is still alive and if you would deign to return with me to Devinagar—to clean out your ancestral home and deal with your family—she might cook her excellent dhansak for you and teach you the samba, the tango, the waltz and Indian filmy dance. She might even talk about the transformation of body parts. And anyway, it is time for Rhodabeh to visit India."

"I would like to ask her about the skeletons of angels," said Erach. "I feel sorry for angels. Carrying around those huge wings on their backs. They must have special skeletal and muscular features like turkeys and vultures. How can they ever dance with complete ecstasy? And if one can't dance, one can't get close to God. Wings tend to get in one's way."

That's when Roxanne Japanwallah named Erach Wadia, "The Ultimate Anatomically-Concerned, Dhansak-Loving Parsi Sufi."

Whenever Erach comes to visit me in Pescadero or I go to

visit him in Oaxaca we cook dhansak. Just the lentil part. We eat it with tortillas. Corn tortillas, flour tortillas, whole-wheat tortillas, blue corn tortillas. And we use cans of Campbell's vegetarian split pea soup that I carry with me from Pescadero to Oaxaca. When I at last went to Devinagar, Roxanne cooked authentic, made from scratch, three types of lentils soaked, cooked and then ground through a colander, daal. As a gift, I took her three jars of La Soledad mole paste that I had bought from Maestra Sofia's nameless store. Maestra Sofia had expanded her store to include a nightly disco-dancing place. After Roxanne and I returned from Oaxaca, Annie and I went to India. Erach and Roxanne had already gone to India. We met them in Mumbai.

I cooked chicken mole in Mumbai to celebrate the friendship between my mother and Señora Rachel that had begun in their respective kitchens in Texas and had lasted till their deaths. And hopefully beyond.

Roxanne and Annie did not let anyone forget that this was to be our "in-search-for-Shireen" journey to India. I didn't even try to dissuade them from their, "Shireen is still alive—somewhere in Asia" conversations. I went because I wanted to visit the city where I was born. I knew that Shireen was dead. Somewhere in Asia.

■■■■■■■■■■■■■■■■■■■■■■■■■■■■■■■■■■■■

The Señora Rachel and Rhodabeh Sohrabji's recipe for Dhansak requested by Erach Wadia.

Daal (Please note: This can be a vegetarian daal. Leave out the meat and add vegetables such as eggplant, potatoes, pumpkin, carrots, zucchini and even spinach.)

Ingredients:
One chicken cut up or a pound of beef or a pound of lamb cut into small pieces. Or vegetables cut up in appropriately sized pieces. Nothing stops you from making a meat plus vegetables dhansak. My mother did it all the time.

> 3 tablespoons vegetable oil
> 2 medium onions, finely sliced
> 3-4 dry red chilies
> 3-4 jalapeño chilies, chopped
> 2 teaspoons allspice
> 2 teaspoons turmeric (in Oaxaca ask for curcuma)
> 2 teaspoons garlic powder
> 1 teaspoon ginger powdered
> 2 teaspoons cumin powdered
> 2 teaspoons coriander powdered
> 2-3 medium tomatoes, chopped
> 2-3 potatoes cut in quarters
> 2-3 carrots cut into small pieces
> 1 can vegetarian split pea soup
> 1 cup of water
> salt to taste.

Method
Combine all the spices and add a bit of water to make into a thick paste. Fry the onions until golden brown. Add the spices and cook for at least five minutes. Add a bit of water if the spice mixture starts burning or if begins to stick to the pan. Add the chicken or meat. Add the green chilies. Cook until the chicken or meat is coated with the spices. Again add a bit of water if needed. Add the tomatoes and the soup. Mix all the ingredients in the pot. Break up any lumps the soup may have. Add water and salt. Cook until the meat is nearly tender. If you have decided to add vegetables this is the time to do it. Cook on medium heat till the vegetables

and the meat are cooked. Add more water if needed. The daal should be the consistency of thick soup that can either be served on top of rice or be scooped up with a tortilla.

Rice
Ingredients
> 2 cups basmati rice
> 2 pieces of cinnamon sticks
> 1 teaspoon powdered nutmeg
> 1 small onion finely sliced
> 3 teaspoons sugar
> 4 cups water
> 4 tablespoons vegetable oil
> Salt to taste

Brown the sugar in a small pan and add one cup of water. Cook until sugar is melted. Keep aside
Fry onions until golden brown. Add rice and mix it with the onions until the rice is coated with the oil. Add the caramel water and blend it with the rice and onions.
Add the cinnamon, the nutmeg, the salt and the rest of the water.
Bring to a boil and then cover the pan. Lower the heat and cook till the water is absorbed and the rice is cooked. About ten minutes.

VARIATIONS AND IMPROVISATIONS ARE HIGHLY RECOMMENDED

Erach Wadia's prompt response sent to me at my Pescadero home consisted of: "Thank you, for the recipes!" and the following quotations.
> *El primer obispo de México, fray Juan de Zumárraga, en su testamento fechado el 2 de*

junio de 1548. . .emancipó. . .al Indio cocinero Juan Núñez, Indio natural de Calicud. . .Zumárraga falleció el 3 de junio de 1548.

Silvio Zavala *LOS ESCLAVOS INDIOS EN NUEVA ESPAÑA.*

The first bishop of Mexico, Juan de Zumárraga, in his will dated June 2, 1548. . .freed his Indian cook, [the slave] Juan Núñez an Indian native [born in] Calicut [India]. . .Zumárraga died on June 3, 1548.

Silvio Zavala *INDIAN (INDIGENOUS) SLAVES IN NEW SPAIN*

And

The word chili is of Nahuatl origin; the plant originally came from the Americas. Thus it is a Mexican export When did chili—or more exactly, the many kinds of chilies—arrive in India and become the essential component of its curries? Did it arrive through the Philippines, Cochin or Goa?

Octavio Paz. *IN LIGHT OF INDIA*

Erach believes in connections and the written word.

Green Kulfi in the Time of Cultivated Vultures

We arrived in India a year before Annie began to demand stories about ancestors.

In Mumbai and Pune we discovered that vultures had become a nearly extinct species and the Parsi community was vigorously debating the issue. Vultures against crematoriums. My mother used to say, "When Parsis argue and debate, it's a good sign. It means that the community is well and alive." She would have enjoyed the debate about the future of vultures. My father said that it was all noise. Homai would have laughed and Ushabehen would have most probably hatke and fatke vultures meri jaan.

Should vultures for the Towers of Silence be specially bred in captivity in Switzerland at great cost to the community? If yes, it appeared that vultures bred in captivity were hand fed and refused to eat human carrion since their breeders hadn't fed them human carrion before they were released. And no one, not even the always gleefully morbid medical students were willing to take on the task of teaching vultures—any vultures—to enjoy humans—dead or alive. Should we build electric or solar crematoriums to dispose of our dead? But then, many of the mobeds refused to come to the crematoriums to perform the ceremonies for the dead. Nor would they perform the ceremonies in the special ceremonial places sanctified for the dead if the dead were cremated and their ashes brought—or not brought—to the ceremonial places. Furthermore some of the mobeds insisted that those who were cremated and had no prayers for the dead performed on their behalf would go straight to hell. I suppose, to meet up with the hell-dwelling Parsi women who had married non-Zoroastrians. And then there were mobeds who performed our ceremonies with deep devotion and compassion that crossed what Homai used to call, "the insanely sketched maps of human beings." As I said, the debate was vigorous. Annie's father, Mr. Foster, the Yupik scholar of Zoroastrianism, took a keen interest in this debate.

The "we" who arrived in India were Annie, Mr. Foster, my father and I. My father had moved to Half Moon Bay fifteen months before we left for India. He had gone beyond his disappointment with my "nimak harami" against the USA and had announced that he wanted to spend the rest of his years in America close to me, his remaining daughter. Besides his on-going long distance discussions with Mr. Foster on nearly every subject one could think of or not think about, he had become engrossed in studying the migration patterns of pelicans who appeared over Half Moon Bay every fall. He visited me at least three times every week and played the piano. "Don't Sit under the Apple Tree with Anyone Else than Me" was definitely not the only song he knew. To play or sing.

When we landed in Mumbai, Erach Wadia, el santo de la India, was waiting for us. He had at last returned to India, after a relentless series of letters and phone calls from Roxanne and was trying to straighten out his family business with mixed success and planned to go back to Oaxaca as soon as he could. He invited me to live with him in Oaxaca. I was thinking over his offer. Max was continuing to make peace with himself.

Surrounded by Parsis—relatives, relatives of relatives, friends of relatives, friends of relatives of relatives—Mr. Foster felt as if he had come home. Especially when he met an old school friend of my father, a gentleman of many years and much gentleness, Behram Ghadially in the Kama Parsi Institute Library. Mr. Foster decided that Mr. Ghadially was the symbol of all that was wise in Zoroastrianism and good in the Parsis. Mr. Ghadially wanted to go to Alaska to visit Mr. Foster's home. But his older sister who at ninety-two continued to narrate the story of how Mr. Ghadially at age seven had lost the one remaining family heirloom, a gold watch, dissuaded him from leaving India. "At your age! The icy wilds of Alaska! Try to be sensible!"

Mr. Foster and Mr. Ghadially spent many hours discussing the questions of conversion to the faith of Mazdayasni Jarthoshtis. Mr. Foster was against it, Mr. Ghadially was for it. My father said that time would take care of the problem. The three men discussed the symbolism of fire, water and plants in Zoroastrianism as well as in some of the indigenous religions of North America until Annie and I told them that they should either co-author a book about symbolism or stop talking about the subject. Mr. Ghadially wrote letters to various newspapers and held forth to whoever would listen about the religious correctness and the moral necessity of crematoriums for the modern world. My father agreed with him. Mr. Foster tended to agree with him but just for the sake of a good debate he took the opposite view. The three men found books and statements in books to support their arguments.

Erach took me to the Bhikkha Behram Well draped with jasmine garlands where Parsis went to pray. He also took me to the Catholic Church on the edge of Bandra where quite a number of Parsi women went once a week to pray to Mary. As we stood outside the church, a Parsi gentleman passing by on the sidewalk yelled at three Parsi women entering the church, "Arré tahme Parsi bairaao taddan jungli cchewo! Tamaroo ketlu nek ane noble religion cchori ne ai gheloo gadoo karo ccho!" At times, he yelled in English. But English or Gujarati, as far as he was concerned, the women were complete fools for forgetting their pure and noble religion by entering and praying in a church dedicated to a European statue. Erach of course tried to persuade him that praying to the Holy Mother in a Catholic Church didn't make the women any less Zoroastrian. The man retorted that no true Zoroastrian prayed to a divine mother who was involved in the absurd and unscientific notion of an immaculate, virgin birth.

"What's wrong with having children the normal way, huh? Ahura Mazda gave us the gift of love and sex. I refuse to give my business to any mobed over the age of thirty who is not married. I don't trust celibate priests or statues that weep." And he huffed off before Erach could regale him with the esoteric knowledge—as he had explained to Roxanne and me—"about the long and respectful history behind the virgin-ness of the Christian Mary which most probably included the narrative of the virgin mother of Mithra—of Anahita. A narrative lost in the battles over land and religions."

I forced Erach to visit every museum and every art gallery in the city with me. But I went by myself to the Parsi Lying-In Hospital where Shireen and I were born and discovered a place of immense calm, dignity and efficiency in the midst of the chaos that is Mumbai. As I stood in the garden, I wondered what my mother had felt when she gave birth to me in this hospital surrounded by trees and flowers where the bird calls of crows and sparrows were infiltrated by the incessant horns of Mumbai drivers. But of course there weren't that many cars in Mumbai when I was born.

The day after my visit to the Parsi Lying-In Hospital, Roxanne arrived from Devinagar and took over our lives. Annie had decided that Roxanne was an ancient spirit and named her, "She Who Must Never Be Tamed." Roxanne in turn decided that "Annie" was too European a name for a Yupik Eskimo and named Annie, Shirbanu, Brave Woman. The two of them accepted their new names in a ceremony at Roxanne's aunt's house on Babulnath Road. The ceremony began with many cups of strong, hot tea accompanied by a variety of snacks and graduated to a lesson by Annie to Roxanne on how to make green Jello with fruit cocktail. The evening ended with Roxanne going off to a train station to make reservations for Annie, Mr. Foster, my father, Erach, herself and me for a four-day visit to Pune. She wanted me to see the city where my mother was born.

Two days later we were on the Deccan Queen traveling through the Western Ghats to the city of Pune. Annie and Roxanne were discussing ways to end wars. Mr. Foster was dozing. Erach was telling me about Shivaji the great Maharashtrian hero. An elderly but definitely spry woman meandered into our compartment in search of a better seat. I had stayed long enough in Mumbai to recognize her as a Parsi especially since she wore her sari the Gujarati Parsi way. Over her right shoulder, brought to the front and tucked into the back to form a perfectly useful cover for her head when and if she needed to cover her head. She found a seat next to a gentleman she seemed to know and at once got into a discussion with him. After a few minutes, everyone in the compartment realized that the discussion had turned into an argument. And the point of the argument became absolutely clear when the woman raised her voice, waved a fist in the air and said, "In the name of Ahura Mazda and all the blessed Asho Farohars, what in this or that world do vultures have to do with religion?" The man next to her yelled, "Everything!" Roxanne of course yelled, "Nothing!" and Mr. Foster tried to intervene with a scholarly and calm discussion, "My dear and learned friend Mr. Ghadially of Karachi who now resides in Mumbai and I feel. . ." He was drowned out by Roxanne, the man and the woman. The argument continued with various members of the compartment— Parsi, Hindu, Muslim and Jain—contributing to it. A Christian gentleman kept on saying, "Burial is imperative. For all of us to rise to meet our Maker on the final Day of Judgment." I thought people would start arguing with him but everyone just nodded at him and continued with the Zoroastrian debate. From the rather acrimonious beginning it turned into a more gentle discussion. Especially when the PARSI DAIRY man appeared selling kulfis. Mr. Foster and Annie, both of whom as we know loved ice-cream in any shape, form or nationality, announced their undying loyalty to pistachios kulfis. Mr. Foster picked up on the death ceremonies arguments and told us how some Native Americans in the USA have a burial custom very similar to the Zoroastrians. But instead of leaving the body in an enclosed Tower of Silence surrounded by orchards, the body is left in a hammock strung between two trees in a designated area. The idea was the same. The body had to be given back as nourishment to the earth and her animals and birds and bugs, to be devoured as soon as possible. When he was a young man, Mr. Foster had seen an ancient and beloved but tragically useless Chevrolet left to rest in peace in one of those funereal hammocks by its grief stricken owner.

The argument died down. The woman who had questioned the role of vultures in religion introduced herself as Perin Dodhi and began a conversation with Mr. Foster and my father. Charmed and intrigued by the two men, she invited us to have "high tea" at her house the next day. Before we got off the train in Pune she gave her address and phone number to Roxanne who it turned out was a distant relative of Perin Dodhi—and I suppose therefore so was I—and asked us if we had any dietary restrictions.

We didn't get a chance to eat any of the multitude of snacks and the tea set out for us by Perin Dodhi the next evening. We didn't even get as far as entering the dining room where we could see a table spread with food and teapots and fine china cups, saucers and plates. The tablecloth and the napkins were embroidered with tulips and daffodils. The dining room was quickly forgotten as we stood in amazement in Perin Dodhi's living room. We had seen enough nineteenth-century over-stuffed British type furniture in Parsi homes not to be surprised by the room's furnishings. The faded and worn out beautiful carpet did not surprise us. We were somewhat surprised that the portrait of Queen Victoria was relegated to a dark corner instead of in the place of honor on the main wall. What amazed us was the nature of the room. It was a shrine. An eclectic one. There were pictures of Zoroaster and the winged Asho Farohars spread throughout the room. There was a beautiful silver filigreed Zoroastrian oil lamp on a table. The room was also filled with pictures and statues of Hindu Gods and Goddesses, suras from the Quran in elegant calligraphy, a prayer rug that looked as if it was used often and the Buddha and Tara in their various forms. The Virgin Mary was very much in evidence. There were pictures of Meher Baba and Sai Baba. A border that spelled out that "God Si Love" adorned the picture of Meher Baba. Annie, my father and Roxanne, of course, mentioned the ghost of E.M.Forster. Erach said that the "si" was most profound if it was a deliberate inclusion in Spanish within the English phrase. A rather large portrait of Madame Blavatsky presided over one corner of the room. Under her was a smaller portrait of Annie Besant. And under that was an embroidered banner that told us that there was Nothing Higher than Truth.

Mr. Foster who had visited New Orleans stated that the only thing comparable to Perin Dodhi's room was the backdrop at the House of Blues where he had attended an unforgettable concert. The music was great but he was constantly distracted by the backdrop with different symbols and words painted all across the canvas. The Om, the Star of David and the Crescent Moon, the Cross, the Virgin of Guadalupe, a Menorah, Meher Baba, Be Here Now, a portrait of Santana and a Zoroastrian Aferghanyu which had bright orange and yellow flames emerging from the silver urn.

Perin told us that her father was a devout Zoroastrian Theosophist. "Theosophists are much maligned," she said. "After all there is nothing higher than truth. Since truth is wisdom, and Ahura Mazda is the Lord of the Light of Wisdom— my father found nothing contradictory about being a good Zoroastrian and a good theosophist. But my special place for prayers and meditation is in that little niche at the back of the room."

The room had no pictures on the wall, no rugs on the tiled floor. There was a table at the far end. Perin took off her sandals before entering the room and we took off our shoes and sandals as we followed her to the table covered with silver vases, tumblers and urns filled with roses. Behind each of these was a photograph. We saw Perin's beloved dead. Her parents, her sisters, her aunts and uncles, her fiancé who had died in Europe during World War II, school friends, friends from college, her father's favorite cat and then there was the photo of Shireen in a silver frame. She was wearing a sari.

There she was, my sister Shireen in a photo. I knew then that my stunned, silent grief, the sound of my father's voice calling out to his younger daughter—once, twice—"mahri nahni dikree, mahri nahlli dikree" and Annie's eyes filled with tears, changing from dark to amber and back to dark would remain with me for as many years as I would live.

Shireen's picture was garlanded with fresh jasmines. Perin Dodhi said, "I always garland this picture with jasmines to remind her that she will have a home with me as long as I live. She loved the smell of jasmines and so I called her Yasmine. She didn't remember her name. All she remembered was that she was born in India. She had that small American flag sewn inside her shirt when I met her. She wore a sadrah-kusti."

"She is my sister, Shireen." I whispered. I tried to laugh but could barely speak above a whisper as I explained, "Our mother always told us to wear clean underwear and a sadrah-kusti whenever we left home. For the usual reasons. 'Suppose you get into an accident. I don't want to think of my daughters being seen in dirty or torn underwear. And how will anyone realize that you are Zoroastrians if you aren't wearing your sadrah-kusti? May God forbid—may nothing inauspicious happen to you—but things happen—and if you die and people don't know that you are

Jarthoshtis then they might bury you in a Christian cemetery. We don't need to take up any space after we die.' And without fail, Shireen would inform our mother that there were only a few hundred people in all of the United States of America who would recognize a sadrah and the kusti for what they were. And the chances that they would be around if we got into an accident were rather slim."

Perin Dodhi had recognized the young woman in the white cotton pants and white loose cotton shirt as a Jarthoshti when she joined Perin in praying three Ashem Vohus and three Yatha Ahu Vaheriyos near a ruined, off-the-tourist-trail, temple in Cambodia. Perin was in Cambodia because her father had believed that one of the greatest spiritual masters of the twentieth century was living in Cambodia. Far from Angkor Wat and the tourists. Perin didn't share his belief but was fascinated by the pictures of Cambodia in one of his books. When she read and heard about the destruction of Cambodia, she decided to go to Cambodia. She didn't know why. Maybe to search for the spiritual master and ask him the reason for wars or the ways to end wars. Instead, she got lost while touring some of the lesser-known temples and found herself surrounded by trees and by old walls. The walls were kept from completely crumbling to the ground by the roots and branches of the trees and vines. She was sure there were snakes around her and began to pray the two prayers she knew would save her from snakes and soldiers. She had just begun the first of her Ashem Vohus when a woman's voice coming from behind her began to accompany her in the prayers. Perin completed her prayers before turning around. She saw two women behind her. A very old Cambodian woman leaning on a stick and a younger woman who could have been from anywhere in Asia west of Japan. She could possibly have been from Italy or Greece. As Perin put it, "Ahura Mazda only knew from where. But she did speak English. At first somewhat rustily." The younger woman was carrying a small plastic bag filled with water with three fish trying to swim in the limited space.

The old Cambodian woman had sheltered my sister when she found her wandering through one of the encampments of Cambodians in the jungle. Shireen was carrying a small American flag and a canteen of water. She was wearing a sadrah with the kusti wound three times around the waist under her ragged uniform. Shireen and the old woman had been together for many years when they found Perin praying for protection. Shireen had forgotten everything from her old life except that she was born in Mumbai. As our mother always pronounced the city. As Shireen had promised us, she remembered the two prayers and kept washing her sadrah kusti which she wore every day.

Perin brought my sister back to Pune. Shireen lived with Perin for about six months. According to Perin she liked to walk around Pune making friends with the children wandering around the town. She said she didn't want to remember anything more than the name Perin gave her, Yasmeen. The flag had disappeared somewhere in Pune right after the photograph of her in a sari was taken. One evening as she and Perin were sitting together quietly after dinner, she said that there was one place she never wanted to forget. The flower market in Pune. It was the most beautiful place on earth and had the most interesting people in it. Shireen died that night in her sleep. Perin had a Zoroastrian funeral for her. My sister was left on the Tower of Silence within twenty-four hours of her death.

My mother would have been at peace. Shireen had come home, to the land of her ancestors, to the land where she didn't have to prove the reality of her existence. And in her death, she hadn't laid claim to even one inch of earth once the vultures, the animals, the insects, the sun and the rain had been nourished by her beloved, beautiful body.